DEADLY HUNT

Strong Women, Extraordinary Situations
Book One

Margaret Daley

Deadly Hunt

Copyright © 2014 Margaret Daley

http://www.margaretdaley.com/

ONE

Tess Miller pivoted as something thumped against the door. An animal? With the cabin's isolation in the Arizona mountains, she couldn't take any chances. She crossed the distance to a combination-locked cabinet and quickly entered the numbers. After withdrawing the shotgun, she checked to make sure it was loaded then started toward the door to bolt it, adrenaline pumping through her veins.

Silence. Had she imagined the noise? Maybe her work was getting to her, making her paranoid. But as she crept toward the entrance, a faint scratching against the wood told her otherwise. Her senses sharp-ened like they would at work. Only this time, there was no client to protect. Just her own skin. Her heartbeat accelerated as she planted herself firmly. She reached toward the handle to throw the bolt.

The door crashed open before she touched the knob. She scrambled backwards and to the side at the same time steadying the weapon in her grasp. A large man tumbled into the cabin, collapsing face down at her feet. His head rolled to the side. His eyelids fluttered, then closed.

Stunned, Tess froze. She stared at the man's profile.

Who is he?

The stranger moaned. She knelt next to him to assess what was wrong. Her gaze traveled down his long length. Clotted blood matted his unruly black hair. A plaid flannel shirt, torn in a couple of places, exposed scratches and minor cuts. A rag that had been tied around his leg was soaked with blood. Laying her weapon at her side, she eased the piece of cloth down an inch and discovered a hole in his thigh, still bleeding.

He's been shot.

Is he alone? She bolted to her feet. Sidestepping his prone body, she snatched up the shotgun again and surveyed the area outside her cabin. All she saw was the sparse, lonely terrain. With little vegetation, hiding places were limited in the immediate vicinity, and she had no time to check further away. She examined the ground to see which direction he'd come from. There weren't any visible red splotches and only one set of large footprints coming from around the side of the cabin. His fall must have started his bleeding again.

Another groan pierced the early morning quiet. She returned to the man, knelt, and pressed her two fingers into the side of his neck. His pulse was rapid, thready, and his skin was cold with a slight bluish tint.

He was going into shock. Her emergency-care training took over. She jumped to her feet, grabbed her backpack off the wooden table and found her first aid kit. After securing a knife from the shelf next to the fireplace, she hurried back to the man and moved his legs slightly so she could close the door and lock it. She yanked her sleeping bag off the bunk, spread it open, then rolled the stranger onto it. When she'd maneuvered his body face-up, she covered his torso.

For a few seconds she stared at him. He had a day's growth of beard covering his jaw. Was he running away from someone— the law? What happened to him? From his disheveled look, he'd been out in the elements all night. She patted him down for a wallet but found no identification. Her suspicion skyrocketed.

Her attention fixed again on the side of his head where blood had coagulated. The wound wasn't bleeding anymore. She would tend that injury later.

As her gaze quickly trekked toward his left leg, her mind registered his features—a strong, square jaw, a cleft in his chin, long, dark eyelashes that fanned the top of his cheeks in stark contrast to the pallor that tinged his tanned skin. Her attention focused on the blood-soaked cloth that had been used to stop the bleeding.

Tess snatched a pair of latex gloves from her first aid kit, then snapped them on and untied the cloth, removing it from his leg. There was a small bullet hole in the front part of his thigh. Was that an exit wound? She prayed it was and checked the back of his leg. She found a larger wound there, which meant the bullet had exited from the front.

Shot from behind. Was he ambushed? A shiver snaked down her spine.

At least she didn't have to deal with extracting a bullet. What she did have to cope with was bad enough. The very seclusion she'd craved this past week was her enemy now. The closest road was nearly a day's hike away.

First, stop the bleeding. Trying not to jostle him too much, she cut his left jean leg away to expose the injury more clearly.

She scanned the cabin for something to elevate his lower limbs. A footstool. She used that to raise his legs higher than his heart. Then she put pressure on his wounds to stop the renewed flow of blood from the bullet holes. She cleansed the areas, then bandaged them. After that, she cleaned the injury on his head and covered it with a gauze pad.

When she finished, she sat back and waited to see if indeed the bleeding from the two wounds in his thigh had stopped. From where the holes were, it looked as though the bullet had passed through muscles, missing bone and major blood vessels. But from the condition the man had been in when he'd arrived, he was lucky he'd survived this long. If the bullet had hit an inch over, he would have bled out.

She looked at his face again. "What happened to you?"

Even in his unconscious, unkempt state, his features gave an impression of authority and quiet power. In her line of work, she'd learned to think the worst and question everything. Was he a victim? Was there somebody else out there who'd been injured? Who had pulled the trigger—a criminal or the law?

Then it hit her. She was this man's lifeline. If she hadn't been here in this cabin at this time, he would have surely died in these mountains. Civilization was a ten-hour hike from here. From his appearance, he'd already pushed himself beyond most men's endurance.

Lord, I need Your help. I've been responsible for people's lives before, but this is different. I'm alone up here, except for You.

Her memories of her last assignment inundated Tess. Guarding an eight-year-old girl whose rich parents had received threats had mentally exhausted her. The child had nearly been kidnapped and so frightened when Tess had gone to protect her. It had been the longest month of her life, praying every day that nothing happened to Clare. By the end Tess had hated leaving the girl whose parents were usually too busy for her. This vacation had been paramount to her.

The stranger moaned. His eyelids fluttered, and his uninjured leg moved a few inches.

"Oh, no you don't. Stay still. I just got you stabilized." She anchored his shoulders to the floor and prayed even more. Even if he were a criminal, she wouldn't let him die.

Slowly the stranger's restlessness abated. Tess exhaled a deep, steadying breath through pursed lips, examining the white bandage for any sign of red. None. She sighed again.

When she'd done all she could, she covered him completely with a blanket and then made her way to the fireplace. The last log burned in the middle of a pile of ashes. Though the days were still warm in October, the temperature would drop into the forties come evening. She'd need more fuel.

Tess crossed the few steps to the kitchen, lifted the coffeepot and poured the last of it into her mug. Her hands shook as she lifted the drink to her lips. She dealt in life and death situations in her work as a bodyguard all the time, but this was different. How often did half-dead bodies crash through her front door? Worse than that, she was all alone up here. This man's survival depended on her. She was accustomed to protecting people, not doctoring them. The coffee in her stomach mixed with a healthy dose of fear, and she swallowed the sudden nausea.

Turning back, she studied the stranger.

Maybe it was a hunting accident. If so, why didn't he have identification on him? Where were the other hunters? How did he get shot? All over again, the questions flooded her mind with a pounding intensity, her natural curiosity not appeased.

The crude cabin, with its worn, wooden floor and its walls made of rough old logs, was suddenly no longer the retreat she'd been anticipating for months. Now it was a cage, trapping her here with a man who might not live.

No, he had to. She would make sure of it—somehow.

* * *

Through a haze Shane Burkhart saw a beautiful vision bending over him with concern clouding her face. Had he died? No, he hurt too much to be dead. Every muscle in his body ached. A razor-sharp pain spread throughout him until it consumed his sanity. It emanated from his leg and vied with the pounding in his head.

He tried to swallow, but his mouth and throat felt as if a soiled rag had been stuffed down there. He tasted dirt and dust. Forcing his eyelids to remain open, he licked his dry lips and whispered, "Water."

The woman stood and moved away from him. Where was he? He remembered ... Every effort—even to think—zapped what little energy he had.

He needed to ask something. What? His mind blanked as pain drove him toward a dark void.

* * *

Tess knelt next to the stranger with the cup of water on the floor beside her, disappointed she couldn't get some answers to her myriad questions. With her muscles stiff from sitting on the hard floor for so long, she rose and stretched. She would chop some much-needed wood for a fire later, and then she'd scout the terrain near the cabin to check for signs of others. She couldn't shake the feeling there might be others—criminals—nearby who were connected to the stranger.

She bent over and grazed the back of her hand across his forehead to make sure her patient wasn't feverish, combing away a lock of black hair. Neither she nor he needed that complication in these primitive conditions. The wounds were clean. The rest was in the Lord's hands.

After slipping on a light jacket, she grabbed her binoculars and shotgun, stuffed her handgun into her waistband and went outside, relishing the cool breeze that whipped her long hair around her shoulders.

She strode toward the cliff nearby and surveyed the area, taking in the rugged landscape, the granite spirals jutting up from the tan and moss green of the valley below. The path to the cabin was visible part of the way up the mountain, and she couldn't see any evidence of hunters or hikers. Close to the bottom a grove of sycamores and oaks, their leaves shades of green, yellow and brown, obstructed her view. But again, aside from a circling falcon, there was no movement. She watched the bird swoop into the valley and snatch something from the ground. She shuddered, knowing something had just become dinner.

Her uncle, who owned the cabin, had told her he'd chopped down a tree and hauled it to the summit, so there would be wood for her. Now, all she had to do was split some of the logs, a job she usually enjoyed.

Today, she didn't want to be gone long in case something happened to the stranger. She located the medium-size tree trunk, checked on her patient to make sure he was still sleeping and set about chopping enough wood for the evening and night. The temperature could plummet in this mountainous desert terrain.

The repetitive sound of the axe striking the wood lured Tess into a hypnotic state until a yelp pierced her mind. She dropped the axe and hurried toward the cabin. Shoving the door open wide, she crossed the threshold to find the stranger trying to rise from the sleeping bag. Pain carved lines deeper into his grimacing face. His groan propelled her forward.

"Leaving so soon." Her lighthearted tone didn't reflect the anxiety she felt at his condition. "You just got here." She knelt beside him, breathing in the antiseptic scent that tangled with the musky odor of the room.

Propping his body up with his elbows, he stared at her, trying to mask the effort that little movement had cost him. "Where ... am ... I?" His speech slow, he shifted, struggling to make himself more comfortable.

"You don't remember how you got here?" Tess placed her arm behind his back to support him.

"No."

"What happened to you?"

The man sagged wearily against her. "Water."

His nearness jolted her senses, as though she were the one who had been deprived of water and overwhelmed with thirst. She glanced over her shoulder to where she'd placed the tin cup. After lowering him onto the sleeping bag, she quickly retrieved the drink and helped him take a couple of sips.

"Why do I ... hurt?" he murmured, his eyelids fluttering.

He didn't remember what happened to him. Head wounds could lead to memory loss, but was it really that? Her suspicion continued to climb. "You were shot in the leg," she said, her gaze lifting to assess his reaction.

A blank stare looked back at her. "What?" He blinked, his eyelids sliding down.

"You were shot. Who are you? What happened?"

She waited for a moment, but when he didn't reply, she realized he'd drifted off to sleep. Or maybe he was faking it. Either way, he was only prolonging the moment when he would have to face her with answers to her questions. The mantle of tension she wore when she worked a job fell over her shoulders, and all the stress she'd shed the day before when she'd arrived at the cabin late in the afternoon returned and multiplied.

Rising, she dusted off the knees of her jeans, her attention fixed on his face. Some color tinted his features now, although they still remained pale beneath his bronzed skin. Noting his even breathing, she left the cabin and walked around studying the area before returning to chop the wood. She completed her task in less than an hour with enough logs to last a few days.

With her arms full of the fuel, she kicked the ajar door open wider and reentered the one-room, rustic abode. She found the stranger awake, more alert. He hadn't moved an inch.

"It's good to see you're up." She crossed to the fireplace and stacked the wood.

"I thought I might have imagined you."

"Nope." As she swept toward him, she smiled. "Before you decide to take another nap, what is your name?"

"Shane Burkhart, and you?"

"Tess Miller."

"Water please?"

"Sure." She hurried to him with the tin cup and lifted him a few inches from the floor.

"Where am I?"

"A nine to ten hour walk from any kind of help, depending on how fast you hike. That's what I've always loved about this place, its isolation. But right now I'd trade it for a phone or a neighbor with a medical degree."

"You're all I have?"

"At the moment."

Those words came out in a whisper as the air between them thickened, cementing a bond that Tess wanted to deny, to break. But she was his lifeline. And this was different from her job as a bodyguard. Maybe because he had invaded her personal alone time—time she needed to refill her well to allow her to do her best work.

She couldn't shake that feeling that perhaps it was something else.

"What happened to you?"

His forehead wrinkled in thought, his expression shadowed. "You said I was shot?"

"Yes. How? Who shot you?"

"I don't remember." He rubbed his temple. "All I remember is ... standing on a cliff." Frustration infused each word.

Okay, this wasn't going to be easy. Usually it wasn't. If she thought of him as an innocent, then hounding him for answers would only add to his confusion, making getting those answers harder.

She rose and peered toward the fireplace. "I thought about fixing some soup for lunch." Normally she wouldn't have chosen soup, but she didn't think he'd be able to eat much else and he needed his strength. "You should try,"—she returned her gaze to him and noticed his eyes were closed—"to eat."

He didn't respond. Leaning over him, she gently shook his arm. His face twitched, but he didn't open his eyes.

Restless, she made her way outside with her shotgun and binoculars, leaving the door open in case he needed her. She scoured anyplace within a hundred yards that could be a hiding place but found nothing. Then she perched on a crop of rocks that projected out from the cliff, giving her a majestic vista of the mountain range and ravines. Autumn crept over the landscape, adding touches of yellows, oranges and reds to her view. Twice a year she visited this cabin, and this was always her favorite spot.

With her binoculars, she studied the landscape around her. Still no sight of anyone else. All the questions she had concerning Shane Burkhart—if that was his name—continued to plague her. Until she got some answers, she'd keep watch on him and the area. She'd learned in her work that she needed to plan for trouble, so if it came she'd be ready. If it didn't, that was great. Often, however, it did. And a niggling sensation along her spine told her something was definitely wrong.

Although there were hunters in the fall in these mountains, she had a strong suspicion that Shane's wound was no accident. The feeling someone shot him deliberately took hold and grew, reinforcing her plan to be extra vigilant.

* * *

Mid-afternoon, when the sun was its strongest, Tess stood on her perch and worked the kinks out of her body. Her stranger needed sleep, but she needed to check on him every hour to make sure everything was all right. After one last scan of the terrain, she headed to the door. Inside, her gaze immediately flew to Shane who lay on the floor nearby.

He stared up at her, a smile fighting its way past the pain reflected in his eyes. "I thought you'd deserted me."

"How long have you been awake?"

"Not long."

"I'll make us some soup." Although the desire to have answers was still strong, she'd forgotten to eat anything today except the energy bar she'd had before he'd arrived. But now her stomach grumbled with hunger.

He reached out for the tin cup a few feet from him. She quickly grabbed it and gave him a drink, this time placing it on the floor beside him.

"I have acetaminophen if you want some for the pain," she said as she straightened, noting the shadows in his eyes. "I imagine your leg and head are killing you."

"Don't use that word. I don't want to think about how close I came to dying. If it hadn't been for you ..."

Again that connection sprang up between them, and she wanted to deny it. She didn't want to be responsible for anyone in her personal life. She had enough of that in her professional life. Her trips to the cabin were the only time she was able to let go of the stress and tension that were so much a part of her life. She stifled a sigh. It wasn't like he'd asked to be shot. "Do you want some acetaminophen?"

"Acetaminophen? That's like throwing a glass of water on a forest fire." He cocked a grin that fell almost instantly. "But I guess I should try."

"Good."

She delved into her first aid kit and produced the bottle of painkillers. After shaking a few into her palm, she gave them to him and again helped him to sip some water. The continual close contact with him played havoc with her senses. Usually she managed to keep her distance—at least emotionally—from her clients and others, but this whole situation was forcing her out of her comfort zone and much closer to him than she was used to.

After he swallowed the pills, she stood and stepped back. "I'd better get started on that soup. It's a little harder up here to make it than at home."

"Are you from Phoenix?"

"Dallas. I come to this cabin every fall and spring, if possible." She crossed to the fireplace, squatted by the logs and began to build a fire. It would be cold once the sun set, so even if she weren't going to fix soup, she would've made a fire to keep them warm.

"Why? This isn't the Ritz."

"I like to get totally away from civilization."

"You've succeeded."

"Why were you hiking up here? Do you

have a campsite nearby? Maybe someone's looking for you—someone I can search for tomorrow." Once the fire started going, she found the iron pot and slipped it on the hook that would swing over the blaze.

"No, I came alone. I like to get away from it all, too. Take photographs."

"Where's your camera?" *Where's your wallet and your driver's license?*

"It's all still fuzzy. I think my backpack with my satellite phone and camera went over the cliff when I fell. A ledge broke my fall."

He'd fallen from a cliff? That explanation sent all her alarms blaring. Tess filled the pot with purified water from the container she'd stocked yesterday and dumped some chicken noodle soup from a packet into it. "How did you get shot?" she asked, glancing back to make sure he was awake.

His dark eyebrows slashed downward. "I'm not sure. I think a hunter mistook me for a deer."

"A deer?" *Not likely*.

"I saw two hunters earlier yesterday. One minute I was standing near a cliff enjoying the gorgeous view of the sunset, the next minute..." His frown deepened. "I woke up on a ledge a few feet from the cliff I had been standing on, so I guess I fell over the edge. It was getting dark, but I could still see the blood on the rock where I must have hit my head and my leg felt on fire."

"You dragged yourself up from the ledge and somehow made it here?"

"Yes."

She whistled. "You're mighty determined."

"I have a teenage daughter at home. I'm a single dad. I had no choice." Determination glinted in his eyes, almost persuading her he was telling the truth. But what if it was all a lie? She couldn't risk believing him without proof. For all she knew, he was a criminal, and she was in danger.

"Okay, so you think a hunter mistakenly shot you. Are you sure about that? Why would he leave you to die?"

"Maybe he didn't realize what he'd done? Maybe his shot ricocheted off the rock and hit me? I don't know." He scrubbed his hand across his forehead. "What other explanation would there be?"

You're lying to me. She couldn't shake the thought.

"Someone wanted to kill you."

TWO

"Kill me?" Shane asked, his mind muddled by the question. The very thought was too much for him to take in. "Why?"

"Have you angered anyone lately?" The woman pushed her auburn hair away from her face and poked at the fire.

When he didn't say anything, she turned from the blaze and faced him.

"I run a company," he said, "so I suppose there are people who aren't too happy with some of my decisions. But to murder me?" He shook his head once and instantly realized his mistake when the room swirled before him. He closed his eyes and waited for the room to stop spinning, then asked, "Why do you say that?"

"What kind of business do you run?"

"Digital Drive, Inc."

Tess whistled. "A company? DDI is a big corporation, so I would say you could have definitely made some people unhappy. DDI is way ahead of its competition, and that might not set well with some of them."

His company was number one in its area, but there were three others not that far behind. He rubbed his forehead, wishing he could massage the pounding away as he tried to wrap his mind around the fact someone might have deliberately shot him and left him for dead. The realization escalated the hammering against his skull. When he reconnected visually with Tess, concern dulled her vibrant green eyes.

"You don't have to play Superman for my benefit. I do know a gunshot wound hurts as does a concussion."

He blinked. "You sound like you've had personal experience."

"I was shot once and have suffered two concussions."

"You!"

"I got in the way of a bullet meant for someone else, but in my line of work, that can be a hazard of the job."

"What do you do?"

"I work for a security agency in Dallas. I'm a bodyguard—usually for people who don't want to call attention to the fact they need one. I have protected female clients, but guarding children is my specialty."

He looked her up and down, noting her small frame, and couldn't believe what she'd just said. She wasn't what most men would consider a beauty, but her mass of reddish brown hair that she had tamed enough to put into a ponytail and her crystal clear eyes that spoke of her straightforwardness were appealing. "I've never met a bodyguard."

"Not that I want a job, but you might need the services of one when you get back to Phoenix." She backhanded a wispy curl from her face. Her creamy complexion was dotted with a few freckles across the bridge of her nose.

"So you think someone is trying to

27

murder me?"

"Yes." Tess swung toward the fireplace and removed the iron pot from the hook. "Mmm. This actually smells good, but then I haven't eaten much today."

The scent of chicken noodle soup spiced the air, laced with an earthy odor, but its aroma—or more likely the fact that he might have someone trying to kill him—roiled his stomach. "I'm not very hungry."

She ladled some liquid into another tin cup while steam wafted toward the ceiling. "Try to get some down. You need your strength. My uncle isn't supposed to join me for several days, and either you'll have to hike down the mountain with me or I'll have to leave you alone for most of the day to get you some help."

"I vote for the second option."

When she smiled at him, the warmth of it reached into the ice he'd packed around his heart years ago. He looked away, but she approached, and her steps eroded more than distance between them. "I agree, but I don't want to leave you alone until I know you can make it without me around." She sat cross-legged near him on the floor while he lay on the sleeping bag. "And I want to check out the area for your—hunters. You wouldn't want them paying you a visit here."

The more he thought about it the more he had to acknowledge Tess was probably right about someone wanting him dead. Although he didn't remember exactly what happened, it was unlikely a hunter had pulled the trigger. He'd rather be cautious than ignore her warnings and be murdered.

So who knew he was going hiking in the mountains? It had been a sudden decision. At work his executive assistant, Diane Flood, was the only one he'd told. She'd been with him from the beginning. It couldn't have been her. But perhaps she'd told someone. His whereabouts wasn't a state secret. Plus, he usually came to this area of wilderness when he wanted to be alone, and a lot of people knew that. And even if someone hadn't known where he was going, it would've been easy to follow him. It wasn't like he'd been looking for a tail.

And what was he even thinking, worried about having been *tailed*? This wasn't his life.

Which brought him back to the question: who wanted him dead? A few rivals popped into his mind. His business could be cutthroat at times, but would any of them resort to murdering the competition? He pictured two of them, Anthony Revell and Mark Collins. Anthony's main offices were in Phoenix. Mark worked out of Los Angeles but often visited his offices in Phoenix. He hadn't made an offer to merge with the company Shane wanted in order to expand DDI's share of the market, but Shane wouldn't be surprised if he did. Neither Anthony nor Mark wanted Shane to succeed with the merger with Virtual Technologies.

"I'm going to lift you up." Tess's husky voice pierced his thoughts. "That way you can drink your soup."

The softness of her touch belied the very idea she protected people for a living. A warm flush infused his face at her nearness. Ever since his wife had died four years ago, he'd kept his distance from women, wanting nothing to do with a casual relationship, while they had thrown themselves at him. They'd seen an unattached rich man, ripe for the picking. He was thankful that his work had given him the direction he'd needed at a terrible time in his life.

While Tess supported his back, he took the cup and tried to bring it to his lips. His arms trembled so much she reached around and stabilized his hands by covering them with hers. Her warmth against them sucked the breath from his lungs until he determinedly shut down his reaction to her.

I'm just grateful, tired and weak. She saved my life. That's all there is. All? He scuffed at the direction of his thoughts. This was a big deal. He made it a point not to depend on anyone. However now, he had no choice but to depend on Tess Miller.

If she hadn't been holding the cup, too, he would have dropped it and scalded himself. Frustration burned a hole into his gut. "I should be able to feed myself," he muttered and let her lift the tin cup to his lips.

"And you will as soon as you get your

strength back. This will help."

After several cautious sips, Shane sagged back against her completely, but she still supported his weight. Exhaustion hovered at the edges of his mind, tugging at him. "I appreciate...what you've done for me."

"You're welcome. More?"

He gave a slight nod and drank the soup, the warm liquid sliding down his throat as his eyelids closed. "I think...that's all."

Sleep descended quickly and whisked him into the blackness.

* * *

After Tess finished eating her own soup, she strode outside with her binoculars and both weapons. Nothing he'd told her had calmed the alarm bells going off in her mind. She didn't like unsolved gunshot wounds, and she couldn't shake the feeling someone was out there watching them waiting for the right moment. But all she saw were oaks, junipers and pinion pines blanketing the landscape, their scent hanging on the light breeze that blew wisps of her hair about her face.

She'd learned in her line of work to be cautious and slightly paranoid. She circled the cabin and the small area where it perched on a cliff at one end of a high country ridge then headed back to the cabin. The sun behind her started its descent toward the horizon. When she reached the door, the hairs on her nape tingled. Again, the feeling of being watched crawled up her spine. She swept one last look over the landscape before going inside.

With a glance toward the sleeping Shane, she quickly crossed the room and withdrew extra ammunition from the locked cabinet and stuffed it into her jeans pocket. If someone were out there, she would be ready for him. After talking with Shane, she had no doubt she needed to carry both of her weapons at all times.

There had been a time when she'd been passive, waiting for life to happen around her. Not anymore, thanks to Uncle Jack. She no longer ran from life or any type of situation, whether dangerous or not.

"Going hunting?"

She whirled around at the sound of Shane's voice, the shotgun grasped in front of her like a shield. "No."

"Then why that?" His gaze veered to the gun, a frown wrinkling his forehead. "Is there some kind of trouble outside?"

I think we're being watched. "Just getting prepared."

"Because you think someone's after me?"

She nodded, seeing the realization in his eyes. "And I think you see the possibility now, too."

"I want to believe it was a careless hunter, but I just can't any longer. Don't you think they're long gone by now? I did go over a cliff when I was shot."

"What if the shooter had been where he couldn't get to you easily? You said it was late when it happened yesterday. Maybe he came back to make sure you were dead. Maybe he followed your trail. It was easy enough for me to find which direction you came from."

"I guess that's a possibility. DDI is close to introducing a revolutionary microchip as well as merging with another company. Let's just say a couple of my competitors would like to beat me to the punch and stop me from strengthening my position in the marketplace."

"How did you find this cabin?"

"I saw smoke. I followed it." He shifted in the sleeping bag and winced.

If he did, so could the person after him, even if some of the rocky terrain obscured Shane's path part of the way. "Do you want some more pain medicine?"

"No, but I could use a drink of water."

She poured some into the tin cup and gave it to him. His hand shook as he drank, but she let him do it by himself. She sensed he needed to feel he could do it himself.

"Thanks." He again adjusted his body, trying to make himself more comfortable on the hard floor.

"I think it's safe enough to move you to the cot if we take it slow and easy." Tess took the cup from him and set it on the table next to the shotgun.

He glanced at the cot a few feet away against the wall. "I'm in your hands."

Tess didn't respond. What she wanted to tell him was that she wasn't responsible for him or anybody. And yet, she was, and there was no way she could deny it.

She positioned herself behind him, squatted and locked her arms around his chest. "Okay. On the count of three help me as much as you can. One. Two. Three."

Aware of the gunshot wound, she carefully hoisted him from the floor. A groan escaped his lips. When he stood, she supported his weight while he slung his arm over her shoulder. She clasped him from his left side so he wouldn't use that leg.

When he lay on the cot, he trembled. She covered him with an extra blanket that Uncle Jack kept at the cabin. But before she could straighten and step away from Shane, he captured her wrist and held her close in a surprisingly tight clasp for someone in such a weakened state.

"Thanks. I've been saying that a lot lately, but I would have probably died if you hadn't been here."

Again, wanting to deny his words, she looked at his face and saw red tinting his cheeks. Listening to him panting after that small exertion, she knew he wouldn't be walking out of the mountains anytime soon. "It was nothing," she finally said and pulled away, his grasp loosening immediately.

He let go of her wrist. "Nothing? I could argue that with you, but it would take too much effort."

"I'm doing what has to be done. Anyone would have."

"Perhaps." His slate gray gaze fused with hers. "Do you always have such a hard time accepting a compliment?" He swiped away the beads of sweat on his forehead, his arm thumping against the canvas of the cot as it dropped back to his side.

"I couldn't let you die." She put a few feet between them. She needed to think of this man as a client, someone to protect. Or a criminal evading the police or other criminals. She only had his word that he was who he said he was. She didn't know what Shane Burkhart looked like. Either way, she needed to don her professional façade.

"Don't shortchange yourself, and I'll ignore the fact you didn't answer my question." He licked his lips. "Can I have some more water?"

When she scooped some out of the container, she noticed she was running low. She frowned as she stared at the few inches of water left in the pot.

"What's wrong, Tess?"

When he said her name, it felt almost like a caress, and her heartbeat accelerated. She quickly squashed any kind of reaction to his smoky timbre. "I'll need to go get some more water at the spring. I think we have enough for this evening, but first thing tomorrow morning, we'll need more."

When she gave him the cup, his fingers, warm against her skin, brushed over hers and sent goose bumps zipping up her arm. She quickly withdrew a few feet.

He downed the liquid. "I never drink this much water." He lost his grasp of the empty cup, and it clanged against the floor.

"Obviously, your body needs it." She stooped to pick the cup up. Her gaze connected to his for a moment before his eyelids closed. He seemed to be fighting to stay awake.

When she studied his face, she glimpsed the paleness beneath the flush to his cheeks. She neared him and grazed her fingertips across his forehead. His skin was on fire, and she snatched her hand back, fear taking hold.

He had a fever, a complication she had hoped to avoid. But she realized that had been a pipe dream. When she'd cleaned his wounds, they'd been filled with dirt matted in the blood around the edges as well as embedded in the injuries.

With a glance at the container of water on the table, she sighed and grabbed her shotgun and flashlight then the handle on the plastic jug. She had to go to the spring. She needed to get water now.

She gave him one quick look, then left, heading behind the cabin and down the slope. The temperature had dropped at least ten degrees as dusk settled over the landscape. She needed to hurry. Even with a flashlight, it wasn't safe traversing out here in the dark. The uneven terrain and sheer cliffs heightened the danger she felt. This far from civilization, there were bears and mountain lions. And most likely a murderer.

At the spring, she clicked on her flashlight to illuminate the path back to the cabin, dark from the overhanging branches of the trees around the area. She quickly scooped up enough water to fill the plastic gallon jug, twisted the cap on tight, and then turned to make her way back. Her foot caught on a rock, and she fell onto her knees. Pain shot up her legs from the hard impact with the ground. She took two breaths and tried to exhale her fear.

She started to push herself to a standing position but stopped when her gaze locked onto a couple of cigarette butts—two to be exact—near the base of a large bush next to the spring. She picked one up and scrutinized it. From the looks of it, the butt hadn't been there long. It certainly hadn't been there yesterday when she'd come for water. The implication escalated her concern they weren't alone.

Using her flashlight, she studied the ground and noticed the footprints. Hiking boots. Only one person. That thought should've relieved her, but it didn't. She knew the damage one person could do to another.

She stepped behind a large bush and looked back at Uncle Jack's cabin. She could see part of the front door. The vegetation was trampled here. The perfect place to stand if someone wanted to watch the door without being seen. Another three cigarette butts lay in the dust near her feet.

Clutching the shotgun in one hand and the water container and flashlight in the other, Tess hurried toward the cabin a hundred yards away. Her heart pounded against her ribcage with each step she took. Someone had been watching her and the cabin. She'd checked the spring out earlier but from the rise twenty yards away. He'd probably hidden behind the bush, out of sight of her survey.

But when she'd circled the cabin earlier and checked hiding places, he hadn't been there. Had he retreated? Come after that?

She'd been armed. Maybe that had scared him off—for the time being.

I won't be caught off guard again. On her job she'd always listened to her intuition. She should have scoured the area more closely until she'd found the intruder, but she hadn't wanted to wander too far from the cabin in case her patient had needed her. Now she didn't know where the assailant was, and she'd be busy and distracted fighting to save Shane's life.

As she approached the door, all her instincts were on high alert. She scanned the terrain one last time before opening the door. At least she could engage the deadbolt tonight while she tried to keep Shane alive.

Just inside the entrance, she froze. She dropped the jug and flashlight, raised the shotgun, and aimed.

THREE

"Step away from him. I have a gun pointed at you." Tess braced her feet apart, prepared to use the weapon.

The intruder slowly straightened, giving her a glimpse of his battered old navy blue ball cap. She sagged with relief. "Uncle Jack! You're not supposed to be here for two days. You just dropped me off in the parking area yesterday. You should have come up then with me."

Her uncle swung around, his bushy eyebrows slashing downward. "Miles from civilization and you still manage to find trouble."

"In this case, trouble came knocking."

She eased the shotgun down and placed the weapon on the table. "And it looks like it could get worse." Snatching up her first aid kit and the water she had already purified, she approached Uncle Jack and gave him a hug. "I'm glad you're here."

"So am I."

Tess turned toward her patient. "He's got a fever."

"Yeah, I noticed. How did he get shot?"

"Good question. He doesn't know. He was on a cliff one second, the next tumbling over the edge. But after what I found at the spring—"

"What did you find?"

"A couple of cigarette butts and a set of footprints behind that big bush by the spring. I'd checked that area earlier and they weren't there then. Someone's after him, and he was watching the cabin. The trouble is, I don't know if I believe his story."

"Which is?"

"He says he's Shane Burkhart, but I didn't find a wallet or any kind of ID on him. So he could be anyone."

Her uncle again examined the man lying on the cot. "I thought I recognized him. He's Shane Burkhart. I saw his photo in the business section of the newspaper a few weeks back about a possible merger. What does he think?"

"He thought it was a hunter until I convinced him otherwise. He doesn't know who's after him." She moved to the side of the co and knelt. "I dropped the water jug in the doorway. Can you boil it for me? I have a feeling we may need it."

"Sure." He grabbed the container and unscrewed its cap as he made his way to the fireplace. "I'll put it on the fire then take a look around. See if I can follow the man's tracks."

"Be careful."

"Tessa, I'm always careful." Uncle Jack winked at her and left the cabin.

She turned her attention to Shane, relieved she didn't have to worry about who he was anymore. One less problem she had to deal with. Shane's groan brought her gaze to his face. He was covered in sweat, heat radiating off him.

"You can't die. I won't let you," Tess whispered.

Think. What more could she do in this primitive environment? Liquids and acetaminophen were all she had to fight a fever. Taking out the bottle of medicine, she mashed three tablets and put them into a cup of water. Somehow she had to get him to drink this.

Sitting on the edge of the cot, she lifted his dead weight, supporting him with one arm while holding the cup in the other hand. At least he wasn't delirious and fighting her. *Thank you, Lord. I need all the help I can get.*

"Come on, Shane. You need this." She prayed her words would reach into his fever-racked mind and make sense to him.

"Elena." He moaned and shook his head, pushing her hand away.

Elena? His wife? No, he'd shared he was a single parent. *Then ex-wife or daughter? Girlfriend?*

Shoving her curiosity to the background, Tess put the tin cup on the floor and tried to secure Shane more firmly against her. When he settled down, she picked up the drink and lifted it to his lips, forcing them open with its rim. At first the water dribbled out of his mouth, but finally, with a lot of gentle coercion and then dire threats of further bodily harm, she managed to get some down him. The front of his shirt and her arm were wet, but she estimated she'd gotten almost half of the doctored liquid in him. She could give him more acetaminophen in a few hours.

After examining the wounds again and finding to her relief that they weren't bleeding, she took a cloth, dipped it into the last of the purified water and bathed his face and neck. She refused to give into the fear building inside. She would not let him die. She would not.

"You listen up, Shane. You'll get well, hear me? You have to."

When Uncle Jack returned, a scowl lined his craggy features. "I didn't see any signs of his assailant." He gestured toward Shane. "The footprints I found at the spring led away from here. But I don't think we should let down our guard."

As much as she didn't like depending on anyone, Tess was glad to hear her uncle say "our guard."

She checked the pot on the fire, removed it and let the boiling water cool on the table. "Why did you come two days early?"

He shrugged. "Last spring we didn't get to spend as much time together as I wished. I'm getting old. I don't put off things like I used to so I told my buddies we would have to reschedule."

Tess sighed. "I came a week early. I should have waited, but I didn't want my boss to give me a long-term assignment and miss this good weather and healing time. There are only so many perfect weeks up here."

"It seems the Lord conspired for us to help this young man."

Tess dragged a chair to the cot and sat. "I guess so, but I was really looking forward to peace and quiet. I get enough tension at work. I prefer my vacations to be relaxing."

"I know, Tessa." Her uncle clasped her

shoulder. "I sometimes miss that life. Mine is too quiet."

She glanced toward him as he shuffled to the table and eased into the other chair. Tired lines cut deep into his tanned face. His blue eyes didn't hold the sparkle they usually did. Retirement wasn't treating him kindly. "Have you thought of doing something with your expertise? Look what you did for me."

He swept his arm down his body. "What? The NYPD didn't need my services any longer. I was forced to retire when I didn't want to. I'm only sixty-three."

"That's my point. You still have a lot of time to do whatever you want. You have a black belt in karate and knowledge in all kinds of ways to protect yourself. You were in law enforcement for forty years. Uncle Jack, you were a captain when you retired. You have lots of information and abilities stored up there." Tess pointed toward his head. "Do something with it besides playing chess and golf. You used to make fun of people who spent half their day at the golf course."

"I'm into bowling now. Golf and I didn't mix. Besides, it gets hot as—let's just say very hot here in Arizona."

"Go back to New York then. You have buddies there."

"Too cold in winter."

She laughed. Her uncle had grown up in Arizona and his heart had always been here, even during the years he'd lived in New York City. He'd been a grump during the winter months when the temperature got below freezing, but his late wife, Patricia, was a New Yorker through and through. She never wanted to leave Manhattan. "I was glad you lived in the city. I owe you so much."

"You're family. What's an uncle for if not to teach his niece how to defend herself?"

"Not all uncles can do that. When I was beat up and left for dead, I decided I wasn't ever going to be defenseless again, and you gave me a way to protect myself—and now others. I make a pretty good living out of all you taught me. I know I've told you thanks before, but I'm telling you again. You gave me a second chance." As she had

Shane, at least she hoped.

Uncle Jack snorted and scanned the room. "Where's the coffee, girl?"

"I haven't fixed any since my guest arrived. I was kinda busy today."

"Well, I guess we better get a pot on because it may be a long night." He pushed to his feet and walked to the fireplace's mantle where the necessary items to prepare what he lived on most of the day were stored.

"Great. Your coffee is much better than mine. I was just waiting for you to show up."

He gave her another snort and finished the task, then took a seat at the table. "So what's your plan concerning our patient?"

Again the word *our*. Although her father was still alive, the very thought of him brought a chill washing through her. He had retired and now lived in a small town outside of Phoenix, but she hadn't seen him on her trips to visit Uncle Jack, and that was the way it would stay if she had anything to say about it. Her dad had bullied her verbally most of her life. As a teenager she'd been timid until a home invasion had left her badly hurt. That was when her uncle had shown up. He'd taken her back to live with him and Aunt Patricia in Manhattan. Her father had been glad to be rid of her.

"Earth to moon."

"Sorry. Just thinking about how much I love you." She knew that would fluster him, and he wouldn't probe too much into why she had been in deep thought. He was the dad she should have had, except her uncle was always trying to reconcile her and her biological father, his brother. But she'd lived under that man's iron rule for too long. Never again. "Tomorrow as soon as Shane is out of trouble, I'll be hiking down the mountain to get help."

"And leave me with him?"

"He won't bite, but our little friend by the spring might. Think you can baby-sit Shane for the day until I can get a helicopter to airlift him out of here? Maybe you can catch a ride home since you're such an *old* man."

The dare, she knew, would rile his temper. With a sharp look toward her, he grumbled something under his breath as he covered the short distance to the fireplace. The only thing Tess heard was "the things I do for you."

"Will you pour me some? It's gonna be a long night."

He poured the coffee and handed her the cup. "I'm going back outside to keep watch. Be useful."

"Don't drink too much coffee. One of us should get some sleep."

"Girl, it isn't going to be me. I don't sleep much anyway, and there's no way I would with someone after him. So I guess you'd better."

She took a long sip, relishing the scent and taste, strong and rich. Then she lifted her chin and stared at her uncle. "Not until his fever breaks. So I guess we'll both be up."

He retrieved the shotgun from the table and with his coffee headed outside, muttering something about how the patient better be worth all the trouble he was causing.

Tess chuckled when the door closed. Her uncle would have been the first person to help Shane. He was always rescuing people and animals. Since he had returned to the Phoenix area three years ago, he'd filled his house and barn with adopted pets. He'd told her the Lord had put him on this earth for that very reason.

She took another sip of her drink, then turned her attention to her patient. She surveyed Shane's tensed features, her fingers combing his dark, wet hair back from his face. Taking the cloth, she mopped away the sweat, only to have it coat his skin almost instantly again. The bond she'd felt earlier strengthened. She'd never forget this man—her stranger. Although she'd had other lives in her hands, protecting someone against a possible threat was nothing like nursing someone back to health. Shane was completely dependent on her. The feeling terrified her, but there was something different, too. Something she couldn't quite name.

After propping him halfway up against the pillow, she poured some water into a tin cup and tried to coax the liquid down his throat, using her fingertips to lightly massage the sides of his neck. His eyes blinked open.

"Come on, drink this," Tess whispered, her gaze locked with his fevered one. "I'm not going to let you dehydrate."

He took several swallows, and then he frowned and knocked the cup away. "I don't know you!" His voice rose louder with each word. His body stiffened.

Although some liquid spilled from the cup, Tess managed to save a little. "Shane, drink," she said in her most commanding tone.

She brought the cup to his lips, but his eyelids slid down and the tension siphoned from him. With the little water left, she got another few gulps down his throat between groans. Then she ran a cool cloth over his face. He batted at her arm, twisting away.

Afraid he would reopen his wounds, she held his limb against his side. "I will not let you die. I will not let you ruin my vacation."

His eyes popped open, and he looked straight through her. "Elena, you came back." A smile graced his lips for a few seconds before he surrendered to sleep.

Do I look like Elena?

Before she could ponder that question, she heard Shane mumbling, "Don't leave me. Rachel needs you."

Now Rachel? Who is that? The daughter?

More questions drenched her thoughts, all involving this man. She needed to get back to Dallas to her simple life where she knew the rules and her boundaries.

Lord, I need You to heal Shane. I've done all I can. Now he's in Your hands.

* * *

After Tess spent hours forcing water, some laced with acetaminophen, down Shane's throat, bathing his face with a cold cloth, and praying like crazy, his fever broke. She sat exhausted, her head dropping toward her chest. Fighting sleep, she jerked up and spied the pot on the fire. Coffee. She needed some if she was going to stay awake and get him the medical and police help he needed.

She headed for the fireplace and filled

her mug. When she turned back toward Shane, his dull gaze captured hers. She went still, waiting to see if he was coherent and aware of his surroundings. He eased his eyelids closed for a moment, then looked at her again.

"Just checking I'm not dreaming," he said, swallowing hard. He lifted his hand and touched his chest. "I'm wet."

"It's a combination of sweat and water. You weren't always as willing to take your sips as I'd hoped."

"Is there someone else here? I thought I remembered seeing a man standing over me." His forehead creased as his gaze scanned the cabin. "I guess I dreamed that."

She shook her head. "My uncle is around somewhere. He comes in every once in a while to let me know that all's well outside."

Shane's attention strayed to an oblong window, set high near the ceiling for privacy. "It's night."

Tess cut the space between them, took a seat, and drank several sips of her coffee.

After glancing at her watch, she said, "It's almost dawn."

"Your uncle's been outside all night?"

"Part of it."

"Why?"

"I found footprints by the spring. Somebody was watching the cabin yesterday."

"So he's been on guard?"

"Something like that." She smiled for the first time in hours. "Truthfully my uncle likes the solitude. When he's up here, he spends a good deal of time outside even at night." She was a lot like that, too.

Shane swiped his hand across his forehead. "So I'm not only indebted to you but now to your uncle as well."

"Don't make it sound like a dose of awful tasting medicine."

"I'm not used to depending on others."

Neither am I. Another link formed between them, deepening their bond.

"You don't owe me a thing. When dawn breaks, I'll hike out of here while Uncle Jack watches over you. By evening, you should be enjoying a nice visit to a hospital."

Shane flinched. "Not something I'm looking forward to. I make a habit of avoiding hospitals."

"I don't think you can this time. Would you like anything to drink?"

He shook his head, but immediately winced at the action. "I forgot my head was split open."

The memories of the two times she'd suffered a concussion crept into her mind. She shoved them away before the doubts took hold. She wouldn't allow those doubts in her life anymore. "How could you forget that? I've had a concussion, and I know how painful it can be."

"My leg hurts even more." He studied her for a long moment. "You've had a concussion as well as a shotgun wound. I remember you telling me that." A shadow entered his eyes. "Your life is full of danger."

She stood and strode toward the door, purposefully ignoring his last statement. Her life before she'd become a bodyguard had been full of a different kind of peril—a peril that threatened the type of person she was. Not only had Uncle Jack and his wife taken her in as a teenager, but also they had taught her about the Lord. Through Him she'd gained an inner strength. "I hope your injuries won't keep you in the hospital long." Stepping outside, she surveyed the area and found her uncle sitting on an out-cropping, as though announcing to whom-ever was watching that Shane had people protecting him. "Uncle Jack, you're a sitting duck."

"I'm fine. I can survey the area better up here."

Tess shook her head. Her uncle had once told her that the Lord looked out for him and he wouldn't die until God wanted him to join Him in heaven. "Shane's awake."

"Coherent?"

"Yep."

Her uncle swung around and came to-ward her. "Good. It should be dawn in an-other half an hour. Then you can boogie on down the mountain."

Although he'd tried to hide it behind a flippant comment, concern laced his statement. "What are you not saying?"

He rubbed the back of his neck. "I've just got that feeling I get when things aren't right. We don't know who we're dealing with, and that always bothers me."

Over the years she'd learned to respect her instinctive feelings. "I'm heading out as soon as it's light enough."

"Great. I'll fix some breakfast." He passed her at the door and went to the food supplies he'd brought. "I'll make some oatmeal and fry bacon. We have to eat it before it goes bad."

"Aren't you supposed to be watching your fat intake?" Tess asked, downing the last swig of her coffee before pouring another cup. Her uncle always brought items to the cabin like bacon even though it meant keeping it cold on the hike up the mountain. He told her once it was a luxury he insisted on having at least for a meal or two.

"Tessa—" Uncle Jack shook his head, tsking, "Tessa, I'm on vacation. Haven't you heard calories and fat content don't count then?"

"I missed that bulletin." She faced Shane, who had been following their bantering. "Would you like some water?"

"No, coffee. The smell is driving me crazy."

"Caffeine probably isn't the best thing for you at the moment. You need rest."

"Didn't you hear your uncle? When you're on vacation, it doesn't count what you eat and, as far as I'm concerned, drink." Slowly, he inched up to a half sitting position.

"Humph." She poured the last of the coffee into his mug, and then handed it to Shane.

As he lifted his drink to his lips, his hand shook, sloshing some of the liquid. He drew in a deep breath. "I think I dreamed about this last night."

"I suppose it's mostly water, so it shouldn't do too much harm."

"After a crack on my head and a gunshot wound, I think a cup of coffee is the least of my worries. Especially with someone out to kill me."

"Which brings me back to, who would

want you dead? Any ideas?"

Shane sipped his drink, staring at the far wall. "I've got two competitors who don't play by the book and are ruthless in some of their practices, especially Anthony Revell. He lives in Phoenix. But the other, Mark Collins, isn't too far away—Los Angeles."

"Okay. How about people who have worked for you? Have you made anyone mad lately?"

"Four hundred people work at my office in Phoenix, not to mention the thousands worldwide. The odds are there are a few who aren't happy with me."

"Anyone threatened you?"

Shane cocked his head to the side, staring off into space for a long moment. "Six months ago, I personally fired one of my researchers. He was stealing information and selling it to the highest bidder."

"He could be the one. Who is he?"

"He's in Mexico. Fled prosecution and disappeared."

"When you get back to town, you need to have the police look into it. And get some protection until you know who shot you."

"You're the only bodyguard I know." While taking a sip, he watched her over the rim of the cup.

She felt the silent question. No, she couldn't guard Shane. This personal connection they had between them was exactly the kind of thing she tried to avoid with her clients. She needed a level of detachment to do her job. Tess barely knew him, but she already knew there was no way she could be objective. After sitting by his bed, struggling to save him, she'd forged a bond with him that could threaten her peace of mind if she allowed him in her life. "I don't think I'm the person for you. You have a security team at the company?"

"Yes."

"Ask your head guy. He should be able to find a person who would work for you."

"I'm a private person. I don't want a stranger guarding me. You aren't a stranger. And right now isn't the best time to let people know someone is after me. I'm in the middle of some delicate negotiations that could fall apart if they knew."

"Your life may depend on it." Even after she said that, from the doubt in his eyes, she wasn't sure if he would pursue her suggestion. She would talk to her uncle about trying to persuade Shane to get protection.

"Breakfast is ready." Uncle Jack brought the pot of oatmeal to the table.

Tess dished up some hot cereal with honey, minus the milk, for herself and Shane. She took him his bowl and assisted him so he could feed himself, then she went back and grabbed a couple of slices of bacon.

When she was finished with her breakfast, she quickly gathered her possessions and backpack for the hike. "I've got to get a move on it if you're to be rescued today. A helicopter would have trouble landing up here at night."

Shane set his spoon in his bowl. "You're going now? Will I see you later?"

"I'll make sure you get the help you need. Uncle Jack will take care of you until the rescuers arrive." She headed toward the door, hurrying before Shane asked another question she didn't want to answer.

She would make sure he was all right before she left, but she needed to cut her ties to him. She motioned for her uncle to follow her outside and waited by the door for him to join her.

During the long night, she'd contemplated what Shane's life was like. When she guarded a person, she made it her business to know all she could about her client. With him, she didn't know much, so she'd filled in the blank spaces. She'd often do that when she people watched. It helped her hone her skills, reading someone's body language—something she'd become quite good at. That had saved her life on several occasions. But in Shane's case, the spaces she'd filled in became more personal. She still couldn't shake the questions—who were Elena and Rachel? Probably his wife and daughter, but she wanted to know for sure.

The fact that she wanted to know bothered her.

"You aren't going to see him again?"

Uncle Jack asked when he closed the door.

"I can't. You need to make sure he understands the gravity of his situation."

"Oh, I will. I have the whole day to work on him."

"Maybe you could even help him find someone to be his bodyguard."

"I'll do some checking when I get home."

"I'll be at your house until I can make arrangements to fly back to Dallas."

"I thought you had the week?"

Tess looked at the closed door and shook her head. "I think I'd better go now. I'll take your car, so you won't have to worry. Call me on my cell, and I'll come pick you up at the hospital."

Her uncle studied her. After a moment, she broke eye contact, but she realized it was useless. He knew her too well. "But you won't even go in to see him again?"

"No."

"Chicken." He dug his set of keys out of his jeans pocket and handed them to her.

"When it comes to relationships and men, yes, I am. Like you, I've seen the darker side of life with our jobs." She cared for Shane, and that was the problem. She waved and started toward the trail that led down the mountain.

* * *

Hours later near the bottom of the mountain, Tess paused and took her binoculars out to scan the area below where her uncle's car was parked. Another one was parked nearby—a black truck. Hunters? Hikers? Or a killer? Although there was only one decent trail that led to the cabin on this side of the mountain, and she hadn't encountered anyone on the path, the assailant might have gone another way. She would check the truck and get the license plate number before she left.

Finally, she neared the end of the trail. Uncle Jack's Jeep was in the lot thirty yards away, just around a bend. She hurried her pace as she turned on her cell phone. She'd tried several times on her hike down, but there hadn't been any reception. She probably would have to drive to the main highway–an hour's drive on a dirt road—before she'd get service.

She reached her uncle's Jeep and scanned the area for the black truck. It was gone. The hairs on her nape lifted. Something wasn't right. She inspected the ground where it had been parked and found cigarette butts littering the earth. The same brand of cigarettes as the ones found at the spring.

FOUR

Tess half leaned, half sat on the deck railing at Uncle Jack's ranch house south of Phoenix, enjoying a cup of coffee and watching birds fly into a twenty-foot saguaro ten yards away. A Gila woodpecker poked its head out of a hole in the cactus, the bright red splotch on the top of it instantly reminding her of Shane's gunshot wound at the cabin only three days before. She knew he would be all right. Her uncle had kept her informed, not just about his progress, but about the number of times he'd asked about her.

It was a good thing she'd cut her ties to the man. Even days later, Shane Burkhart dominated her thoughts more than she wished. She kept telling herself it was because she'd saved his life, but in her line of work, she'd saved plenty of lives, and that hadn't caused her to dwell on their image or go over the words they'd exchanged. But Shane ... she couldn't forget the steel gray of his eyes, his muscular build, his unruly dark hair ...

The blare of a police siren startled her, pulling her mind from her memories of a man she needed to forget. She answered the special ring tone on her cell phone that indicated it was Uncle Jack. "I thought you'd be out of cell range by now."

"Nope. Almost to the bottom of my mountain, though. Turned off the main highway five minutes ago. Did you decide to stay longer? There's no reason to go back to Dallas so soon. You still have vacation time, and you could always come back to the cabin."

It might never be the quiet, peaceful retreat it used to be. "Not this time, but I'm staying at your ranch until it's time to go home." She nearly stumbled over the word *home*, because she really didn't have one. The apartment she shared with another female bodyguard was hardly more than a place to sleep and warm up a can of soup. They rarely saw each other, since their schedules were so different. "I'll keep Charlie in line," she said in reference to the only cowhand her uncle employed.

"Your dad's place isn't too far away. You ought to pay him a visit. Find some resolution with him."

She shivered at the thought of seeing her father, the memories of his angry, wounding words. "Not gonna happen. And you know why."

"You need to forgive him, so you can move on."

Tess released a long breath. Deep down, she knew he was right. "I don't know if I can. You should have been my dad. In every way that matters, you are."

"There's a reason the Lord wants us to forgive."

She was desperate to change the subject. "When's Shane leaving the hospital?"

"Why don't you go see him and find

out?"

Tess rolled her eyes and looked skyward to see a hawk overhead. Brilliant. She'd changed the topic to another one she needed to avoid. Her uncle had tried to get her to see Shane for two days.

"Still there, Tessa?"

"You wouldn't return to the cabin if he wasn't going to be okay, and I'm sure he's got plenty of family and friends looking in on him. Why do I need to visit him?"

"I didn't save his life. Don't you want to see how well he's doing?"

"My job is over. I saved him. I'm letting the doctors take care of him now."

"Not every marriage ends like your parents' did."

Suddenly Tess felt twelve again, watching the gurney being rolled out of her home. The sheet flapped in the wind, covering the body that used to be her mother. Tears pricked Tess's eyes. She blinked and tried to push the mental picture away, but the memory of her father's insults bombarded her.

"I don't want to talk about my parents."

Her mother committed suicide, leaving her alone with a father who didn't want to be one.

"I was happily married for thirty years."

"Patricia died, and you shut down. I wasn't sure you'd ever come out of your depression. So no, thank you. The divorce rate is sky high. I don't want to add another number to it." *How in the world had they gotten on the subject of marriage?*

Uncle Jack snorted. "Chicken. I didn't think you feared anything. Now, I know you do."

"Nice try. It isn't going to work. Enjoy your time at the cabin for me. I'm going to kick back here and relax. Maybe go riding. See a few friends who still live here."

His robust laughter filled her ear, and she pulled her phone away until he quieted. "I have friends here and in Dallas."

"You're in Phoenix maybe twice a year, if I'm lucky. I suppose you're in Dallas a little more, but not much."

"I go where the job takes me. Will you be back before I leave?"

"Yes, I've got to spend a couple of days

with my gal."

Although she knew her uncle loved to hunt at this time of year, she wondered if he was giving her a chance to reconsider helping Shane. "Love you, Uncle Jack. See you in a week."

When she disconnected, she stuffed her cell phone in her front jeans pocket, took a deep breath of the fresh air—its scent different from Dallas—and went back into the kitchen. She headed for the coffeepot, refilled her mug and started for the deck again.

The doorbell rang. She changed directions and made her way to the foyer. Wondering who was at the door, she checked out the peephole and frowned.

Why is he *here?*

She stepped away and debated whether to open the door or not. Uncle Jack's earlier taunt about being afraid of Shane mocked her, and she reached for the knob. When she opened the door, her gaze locked with Shane's, a gleam in his eyes as if he'd seen her hesitation. She remembered those beautiful eyes—hard to forget that steel gray—but nothing could've prepared her for his mesmerizing look.

She stared, dumbfounded, until he broke the silence. "May I come in?"

She mentally shook herself and opened the door wider. Every instinct shouted for her to slam it in his face and lock him out. Too much idle time on this vacation—it was messing with her nerves. And this was why she worked more cases than any other bodyguard at the agency—she needed to stay busy. To stay detached. Alone.

He entered, leaning heavily against a cane, and brushed past her. One of his hands clutched a brown paper bag.

When he paused, scanning the foyer, she gestured toward the sack. "What's in there?"

"Lunch."

"What if I've already eaten?"

"Then I wasted my money. Have you?"

A *yes* was on the tip of her tongue, but she couldn't lie, especially not to him. "No."

"Good. I brought your favorite sandwich from your favorite Phoenix café."

Surprise widened her eyes. "What?"

"A spicy taco sandwich from Pete's Deli."

"How did you know?"

"Jack."

Suspicion pinched her mouth as she narrowed her gaze on him. "What else did you ask him?"

"Why you didn't come to the hospital to see me."

She was going to wring Uncle Jack's neck when she saw him. "What did he say?"

"That I needed to ask you. Then he gave me directions to his ranch and told me I should bring you that sandwich. I happen to like Pete's Deli too, so I also got us both something."

She poked her head outside and surveyed the front yard, noting a Lexus but nobody else. "You came all this way by yourself?"

"I'm a big boy, and the doc okayed me to drive."

She huffed. "Somehow I get the feeling even if he didn't, you'd do what you wanted. You do realize there's a killer out there after you?"

"Yes." He glanced down at his leg and the cane, then met her eyes with a smile. "Now, where do you want to eat?"

His determination reminded her of herself. No wonder he was the head of a multi-million dollar corporation.

"Out on the back deck. Would you like coffee?" She moved toward the kitchen, her stomach rumbling with hunger at the mention of her favorite sandwich. She decided she would hear him out, and then send him on his way.

"That's fine. I like mine black."

Just like me. What other similarities did they have? She filled a mug for him, then held the back door open for him to maneuver through the exit to the wraparound deck. "The table and chairs are this way. The eastern view is better." Her attention latched onto the mountains in the distance, and she thought back to when she'd met Shane. Who was after him? Why? And why wasn't he more concerned? Did the police have a lead? She intended to find out.

After Shane settled into a chair at the

round glass table, he placed his cane on the deck and opened the bag. "I brought you two of them."

She'd kill her uncle, telling Shane she always ate two. But how often did she get Pete's? "Uncle Jack ratted me out, huh?"

"No, it was just a hunch."

"Really? Do I look like I overeat?" She slid his mug across the table to him. "Wait. Don't answer that."

"Don't be ridiculous. I'm not sure why, but it felt right to get you two. I always have seconds of something I really enjoy."

After blessing her food, she took a bite of her sandwich, savoring the spicy flavor of the taco meat mixed with lettuce, toma-toes and cheese. "No one makes it better than Pete. I've been going to his deli since I was a kid."

"So, you grew up here?"

Give her a taste of one of her favorite foods, and she might just tell him her whole life story. His question put her on guard, though. She didn't go down memory lane, even with Uncle Jack when she could avoid it. "Yes. Where did you grow up?"

"Back East. That's where I sent my daughter yesterday—to stay at my parents' estate."

"You mentioned her at the cabin? How old is she?"

"Fifteen. She wasn't too happy, but I didn't want her here in Phoenix until the police discover who shot me. I hired a bodyguard from your agency to guard her. Although the security at my parents' estate is excellent, I'm not taking any chances."

"Is her name Elena or Rachel?"

His brow furrowed. "Rachel. How did you know?"

"You said both of those names in your delirium. Is Elena your wife?" She cringed, horrified she'd asked the question that had been plaguing her for days. Did she really want to know?

"She was. She died four years ago." Neither his expression nor his tone revealed what he was thinking.

"I'm sorry." She took another bite of her sandwich, and then washed it down with a swallow of her coffee.

"So am I." He stared off toward the

mountains to the east. "She's with the Lord now."

A moment of silence fell between them, but it wasn't uncomfortable. The urge to console him swamped Tess, and she gripped the arms of her chair to keep from reaching across the table and covering his hand. "Why are you here?" she finally asked, needing to end this meal and send him on his way.

"I need your help. When I arranged a bodyguard for Rachel, I checked to see if I could hire you to be my bodyguard. Your employer said you were on vacation and that she wouldn't force you to end your vacation early. So I'm here asking. Will you?"

This time of year the temperature was cool and only in the seventies with a light breeze blowing, but perspiration coated her upper lip and palms. The idea of guarding him set her nerves on edge. She'd always felt safe at Uncle Jack's ranch, but with Shane here, knowing someone wanted to kill him, she felt very exposed. He'd finished his food, and she couldn't stomach another bite. "Let's go inside."

As he hobbled toward the back door, Tess cleaned up the trash and then hurried after him. Before entering, she paused and glanced over her shoulder. The hairs on her nape prickled, and a shiver snaked down her spine.

"Let's go into the office." Probably the safest room downstairs, with its one window. Funny. A few minutes ago, she'd been a gal on vacation. Now, her bodyguard persona had taken over. She pulled the blinds while Shane sank onto a chair in front of the desk. She sat beside him. "I can't do it. I'm not on top of my game. I need a rest."

"Your employer said that if you take the assignment, she'll extend your vacation after the job. I'll pay for an extra week, too."

"Why me?"

"Because I saw you in action, so to speak. You saved my life. I wouldn't be here if I hadn't stumbled upon that cabin. You and I both know that. I had my head of security at DDI check into you, and you have an excellent reputation."

"Don't you have security at DDI who can help you?"

"They aren't bodyguards, and I don't want anyone at the company to know I have one. I'm in the middle of some important negotiations, and if word got out that someone is trying to kill me, everything could fall through. I don't want to risk that."

"So how are you going to explain me?"

"Since I'm injured, I'm going to work from my house. Everyone will think you're the woman I'm dating. I have a few engagements I must attend, and that way you can go as my date."

"And the other times?" Why was she asking questions, when she knew she should say no?

"A concerned girlfriend taking care of me. The head of my security, Neil Compton, has made sure my security is topnotch at my home."

"You don't have staff at your house?"

"Yes. A housekeeper and a groundskeeper. They're a couple."

"Then it might be strange that I'm staying at your place."

"There might be speculation, but it

won't affect the negotiations. When the person who is after me is caught, it won't make any difference. The police are working the case quietly."

"What have the police learned?"

"Not much. Both Anthony Revell and Mark Collins have an alibi for the time of the shooting."

"But they could have hired someone, so that doesn't mean much."

"I'm pushing to get these negotiations completed. I'm hoping DDI will merge with Virtual Technologies, but the VT's board has been stalling since my *accident*. I'm going to a dinner at the VT's president's house in three days. We should close the deal shortly after that. But first, I have to prove to them that I'm on top of my game, despite ..." He indicated his bandaged leg and the cane, leaning against Uncle Jack's desk.

"Are you?"

"I'm healing, and except for a dull ache in my leg I can tolerate, I'm fine. Nothing vital was damaged. I'm even hoping to give up the cane by then." He tilted his head to the left. "So will you help me? I'm asking for four or five days until the deal is finalized, then I'll hire a different bodyguard to follow me around, if I still need one."

She rose and crossed to the window to peek out between the slats in the blinds. Charlie exited the barn leading a chestnut horse. Uncle Jack's cowhand wasn't much younger than her uncle. She'd always enjoyed the time she'd spent with him riding over the rugged terrain checking on the fences and the couple of hundred head of cattle. If she took the job, she'd miss that this vacation.

The scrape of a chair against the tile floor sounded behind her. She sensed Shane bridging the distance between them, but she didn't look at him. Part of her wanted to help him. Heaven knows he needed it. But the other part demanded she refuse—and not because she couldn't do it. She didn't understand this hesitation. She rarely turned down work, but ...

Only inches away from her, Shane leaned toward her and said, "Please. I'll make it worth your time."

It wasn't about money. No, it was about

the way her heartbeat sped up even now. How was she going to keep this relationship professional when her body went all haywire at his very nearness? She breathed in his scent of sandalwood, and was filled with a sudden fear for this man. Her mouth went dry. He needed to be protected, and she didn't know if she could do it. She had to swallow several times before she could deny him.

But she made the mistake of sweeping around and stepping back to allow more room between them. Their gazes fused, and she felt bound to him, responsible for his safety. He was only there now because she'd saved his life.

The corner of his mouth quirked. "Will you, Tess?"

Her name on his lips was like the comfort of a soft, warm blanket. Chills raced up and down her arms, leaving goose bumps.

"Yes."

His grin weakened her knees. She sank against the windowsill, drinking in his smile.

"Can you start right now?"

Right. Work. She shook off the feelings and gathered her professional façade. This was a mistake, but if anything happened to him, she wouldn't be able to forgive herself. *God, I'm going to need You on this assignment.*

"I'll wait for you to pack something. You can follow me, if you want."

"No, I'll be going in your car."

"But—"

She held up her hand, palm toward him. "If I'm going to guard you, you have to agree to do everything I say. No questions. There may come a time when there won't be any time for debate."

"Okay."

"You driving here by yourself was a stupid thing to do. You exposed yourself, and for all you know, your killer is right outside, waiting for you to walk out."

"You didn't give me a choice, Tess. You never came to the hospital."

"I hate hospitals." *And I was avoiding you.*

"Like me."

Another thing they had in common. She

hated them because, as a teenager, she'd spent four days in one after those thugs had broken into her home and beaten her senseless. What was his reason? No, she didn't want to know. Business only—nothing personal. "Remember, you do as I say," she said in her no-nonsense voice.

"I've already agreed to that."

She wasn't totally convinced she should take this job, and she wouldn't continue if he didn't listen to her. She'd dealt with men like Shane, men who were leaders, not followers, and they always felt capable of protecting themselves. Their arrogance made them vulnerable. "Wait in here. I'll be back in a little bit, and then we can leave."

* * *

Shane watched her walk away, finally letting down the pretense that he was all right. His wounded leg throbbed, and this excursion had exhausted him. A little blood loss and he felt woozy. Okay, it was more than a little blood loss, but he'd never been a good patient.

The only reason he'd agreed to this arrangement was because his head of security had insisted that he have a bodyguard and that he curtail his activities. Rachel had concurred and said she would behave if he hired a bodyguard, too. He couldn't take a risk with his daughter. He'd lost his wife to a reaction to an antibiotic that caused her body to dump her sodium. Rachel was his whole world.

After Elena died four years earlier, he'd thrown his energy into his company. But in the past few days, with his near death, he'd realized he had a lot to make up for with Rachel. And he would, once the person trying to kill him was caught.

"Are you ready?" Tess asked from the doorway into the office. She clutched a bag in her hand.

"That was fast."

"Clothes, weapons, ammo. I've got all I need."

"Weapons?"

"I carry several in case I need them. I always have two with me. Right now, one's in my holster. The other's in my purse. Do you know how to shoot?"

"Yes."

"Do you have a gun?"

"I lost my rifle when I fell from the cliff."

She started toward the foyer. "Do you hunt? Was that why you were in the mountains?"

"No. My daughter would disown me. I carry it for protection in case I come upon a mountain lion or a bear."

"Or a person trying to kill you."

He reached around her and opened the front door. "Or that."

"You're taking this pretty calmly." She held up her hand to halt him from coming outside, then she scanned the area before motioning him to leave her uncle's house.

"In the business world, especially when conducting negotiations, I've learned to keep my feelings private." *Probably too much*. Elena had complained she didn't know what he was thinking half the time, even though they'd been married twelve years when she died.

He stored her duffel bag in the trunk of

his Lexus. While Tess slid into the front passenger seat, he climbed behind the steering wheel and slanted a look toward Tess. She surveyed the landscape, and by the alert expression on her face, she had slipped into her protective mode while packing—actually even before that. In that second, he knew he was in capable hands, and that thought relaxed him.

As he drove away from the ranch, he played through what he'd discovered about Tess when he asked his head of security to investigate her and Jack Miller. Her credentials were impeccable, and her uncle had been a police officer in New York for decades before he retired. As far as he could tell, Tess devoted herself to work. He could identify with that. Actually, there was something about Tess that made him feel comfortable—the same as he had with Elena when he'd first met her at college.

"Do the police have any idea who is after you?"

Her question dragged him away from the past. "I gave them all the names I could think of. Until this happened, I never thought there could be someone who'd want me dead. But I have to be honest with myself. I've made a few enemies in my work. I've taken over companies that resented it, although they are better off under my management."

"Some people can't stand not to be in control. Anyone in particular or connected to this most recent merger?"

"There's one guy on the board of Virtual Technologies who has been vocal. He's trying to get the votes to stop the merger."

"Who?"

"Chase Temple and he has a few allies supporting him." Shane turned onto the curvy part of the two-lane road between the ranch and the outskirts of Phoenix. "I don't know that I would like to travel this road at night. It must be pitch black except for your headlights."

"Yeah, I've told Uncle Jack that a couple of times, especially the time I encountered a deer leaping across the highway. I swerved to miss it and ran off the road into the cacti. But my uncle loves the quiet and isolation."

"And he lived in New York City for years?"

"I think he loves the isolation because he did live there."

As Shane took another sharp curve, he saw something on the side of the highway.

Tess held up her hand. "There's something across the road."

FIVE

Shane stomped on the brakes while Tess swiveled her attention to the roadside. Tension whipped down her body as she drew her gun from the holster at her side. Two men dressed in black, faces covered with ski masks, ducked into the brush on the left. But not before she glimpsed their weapons.

The tires thumped as the Lexus drove over a barbed chain that had been thrown across the road. The car slowed, coming to a stop a few yards away from the spiked roadblock.

Tess yelled, "Get down," as a shot hit the driver side window. "Stay put and call

911."

Tess, hunkered down below the window, opened her door and slipped out of the car. Adrenaline surged through her as she low walked toward the front of the hood. When another shot blasted the air, she popped up and returned fire, sending the masked thugs into a ditch. Tess scrambled toward the rear of the Lexus to keep the two assailants guessing.

As she got off another round, in the car Shane poked his head up and squeezed off a shot. He must've grabbed the spare weapon in her purse. Tess gritted her teeth. What part of *stay put* did he not understand?

A bullet whizzed by her head, then another shattered the side window behind Shane. Their assailants continued raining bullets down on them as though they had an endless supply of ammunition. Tess didn't. On her, she had one extra clip while the rest of her ammo was in the duffel bag in the trunk.

She heard a distant siren coming from the south and thanked God that help had been close by. Suddenly, the two men burst from their hiding place and, with guns firing repeatedly, made a mad dash toward a dirt road a hundred feet north of their position. Tess wanted to go after them and put an end to this, but her primary job was to protect Shane. After getting off a couple more shots, she squatted by the hood of the Lexus until finally, silence reigned.

The sound of another siren, further away, came from the north. She peered around the front and saw a black pickup truck. It looked like the one that had been parked next to Uncle Jack's Jeep when she'd hiked down from the cabin. The truck zoomed out of the dirt road and sped north. She tried to read the license number, but mud obscured it. All she could see was that it was a New Mexico plate. As the pickup disappeared from view, she checked on Shane. When she climbed into the front seat of the Lexus, her heartbeat pulsated against her skull from the gunfire exchange.

Shane slowly straightened from a slouch, her Glock still in his hand, shattered glass sliding off him. He looked at her, his face pale. She took her gun from him and stuffed it back in her open purse.

She had a few words for Shane, but she clamped her lips together as one of the sheriff's cars arrived from the south. She stepped out of the Lexus, holstered her weapon, and walked around the car. All four tires were flat. Bullet holes riddled the white finish. If there'd been any doubt about someone wanting Shane dead, it was gone now.

Shane exited his Lexus as a deputy walked toward them. Tess relaxed for the first time. She knew the man.

"Are you Mr. Burkhart?" the officer asked as he took in the Lexus as if it had been in a war zone.

"Yes." Shane took out his wallet and showed the deputy his license.

"You called 911?" When Shane nodded, the deputy continued. "What happened?"

Shane pointed at the spiked roadblock stretched across the pavement. "I couldn't stop in time. Two men over there," he indicated the area, "fired on us. When they heard your siren, they ran off that way." He pointed north to the dirt road, obscured partially by the vegetation. "Got into a black pickup and took off north."

"Good thing I was nearby when I received the call." The deputy, a friend from high school named Brady, shifted his attention to Tess and smiled. "Are you on a job?"

"Yes. He hired me today. We were leaving Uncle Jack's and going to his house."

"Is Jack at the ranch? You aren't going anywhere in that car." Brady blew out a slow whistle as he inspected the Lexus again.

"No, he's in the mountains."

A second patrol car from the north pulled up, and Captain Paul Daniels exited his vehicle. He was a good friend of Uncle Jack's, but then he knew a lot of the law enforcement officers in the area, especially Maricopa County's District Six.

"Maybe you or Paul could give us a ride back to the ranch. I can use my uncle's truck." She nodded toward the captain, who stopped next to her.

"I'll do that, Brady, while you process

the crime scene." Paul pushed his cowboy hat up on his forehead and examined the Lexus. "Tess Miller, trouble follows you everywhere. It's good to see no harm was done to you two. Not from lack of trying, from the looks of this car."

"Tess, did you or Mr. Burkhart get a look at the assailants?" Brady moved toward the area where the attackers had hidden.

"They had ski masks on, but one was about six feet and the other five nine or ten. Both had a stocky build. Paul, you should have passed the black truck as you came down the road."

The captain squinted north. "Nope, but there are several other dirt roads they could have turned onto. I'll have another deputy check them out. Did you get a license number?"

"No, but it was a New Mexico plate. The numbers were covered except"—Tess visualized the speeding truck—"the last number was nine, I think."

"At least that's something to go on." The captain pulled out his cell phone and placed a call.

Brady continued his trek toward the area where the two assailants had hunkered down in a ditch that had offered them some protection from Tess's return fire.

While Shane talked with Captain Daniels, giving him more details of what went down, Tess followed Brady. Her friend examined the ground, careful not to disturb any evidence, while Tess stood back on the pavement.

Brady crouched down even further. "Looks like blood. Did you hit one?"

"I don't know. Everything happened fast. Most of the time I was pinned down. But if that's human blood, it's most likely one of the assailants."

Brady grinned up at her. "Then we may be able to track him down. *If* he's in the system."

Tess looked to where the two thugs had first hidden before she exchanged fire with them. A cigarette butt, leaning against a bush and partially in the dirt caught Tess's attention. "Look at that, Brady. It might belong to one of the assailants. This isn't the first time someone tried to kill Shane."

Brady sat back on his heels and looked at her, his eyebrows raised. She told him the story of what had happened on the mountain.

When she was finished, Brady nodded toward the cigarette butt. "Good. Another piece of evidence we might be able to use. From the looks of that Lexus, these scumbags meant business. I'm glad Mr. Burkhart hired you."

She glanced back at the shot up Lexus. When she thought of what could have happened if Shane had been alone returning to his house, Tess shivered.

* * *

Late that afternoon, Tess entered Shane's mansion. Just the foyer of his house was the size of half her apartment in Dallas. Straight ahead, a grand staircase of rich mahogany swept to the second floor. A matching round mahogany table stood in the center of the marble floor near the entrance. A large bouquet of fresh flowers, various varieties in many colors, drew

Tess's gaze. Their sweet fragrance sprinkled the air, making her forget for a few seconds why she was here.

She circled the entry, peering into an elongated living room, decorated in an elegance that complemented the dining room, which lay across the foyer. Twelve people could sit at a massive table and enjoy a meal together.

"My wife decorated this area to entertain business associates. I rarely use these rooms. Come on. I'll show you around before I take you to your bedroom."

Tess looked at the rooms one more time. "Your wife had good taste."

"Yes, Elena did."

She followed him past the staircase, down a long hall, and into the den.

The first thing Tess saw was a beautifully carved dark mantel with a portrait of a stunning woman with auburn hair. Elena. "How did she die?"

He stared at his wife's portrait. "A drug reaction. All my money, and I couldn't do a thing to help her. Her sodium level plummeted, and the doctors couldn't turn it around. I was on a business trip. As soon as I heard she'd been taken to the hospital, I came home as fast as I could." He swallowed hard. "I didn't make it in time. I should have been there for her. The housekeeper found her delirious. If I'd been here, I might have been able to get her help in time." He blinked several times and wrenched his gaze away. "I don't usually share that story, but with all that has happened in the past days ... "

"I guess getting shot at would bring a lot of things to the surface."

"You were in danger today because of me. Maybe this isn't such a good idea."

She held up her hand. "It's my job to protect you."

"I know, and I'm alive today because you did, but I can't take another person's life in my hands."

"Is this because I'm a female? Would you have said that if I were a man?"

He studied her for a long moment. "Elena had the same color hair as you do." His attention swiveled to the portrait. "I didn't think about it until now. I—"

Tess stood in front of Shane. "We look nothing alike except for that. There are a lot of people with auburn hair, but if you want to get another bodyguard, I understand. I won't leave, though, until the replacement shows up."

Shane shook his head. "No. I just think what happened this afternoon is finally catching up with me. I learned two things today. First, someone definitely wants me dead. Second, you're certainly capable of protecting me."

Tess nodded her acknowledgement. "Where's your housekeeper? I want to meet her and then finish the tour."

"Probably in the kitchen, fixing dinner. She and her husband have a suite of rooms off the kitchen. C'mon. I'll introduce you, then show you where you'll be staying."

"I want to be in the bedroom next to yours."

"That's fine. I thought you might and had Anna prepare it for you."

"You were that sure I would accept?"

Using his cane, he limped toward the hallway. "No, but I did a lot of praying that you would. I know when I need help. My expertise is in computers, not protection. That's why I promised to do what you say."

Staying where she was, Tess pressed her lips together. When he turned at the entrance and saw her standing there, one of his eyebrows arched.

"This is what it looks like to stay put. Earlier today, you returned fire. That was my job, not yours. I know what I'm doing."

He strode back to her, his arm stiff at his side while his fingers curled then un-curled. "I know how to shoot, and if a gun is available, I'm capable of helping. If you need a demonstration of my abilities with a weapon, I'll be glad to give you one. I often hike in remote places, and I always carry a gun as protection and hope I never have to use it." His bearing gave off waves of self-assurance as though he were in a board-room issuing orders to his employees.

"Then why do you need me?"

"I'm no expert, just because I can fire a gun. I will do as you say unless I don't see the logic in it. I respect your abilities, but that doesn't mean I can't *help* defend myself. I won't be a passive client. Do you have a problem with that?"

Her first impulse was to head for the door and return to Uncle Jack's ranch. She scanned the den while trying to calm the anger bubbling to the surface. Her attention landed on a photo of Shane with a teenage girl who had his coloring but looked like Elena. The picture of him with his daughter melted her irritation. She'd dealt with worse clients, people who continually got in her way. She could deal with him. She wouldn't let anything happen to him, because Shane was the only parent Rachel had. That was motivation, if nothing else, but after what happened on the highway earlier, she wouldn't have walked away, even if he were childless.

She returned her focus to him. "Then I suggest we get to know each other, because this won't work if we're second guessing each other."

"Agreed. And you are the expert, but I'm not helpless."

She smiled. "Even when you were in the cabin, I knew you weren't helpless."

A sparkle gleamed in his gray eyes. "If a wounded man stumbled into my cabin with cuts and bruises and torn clothes, that wouldn't be the first thing that would come to mind for me. I bet there was a time you thought I was probably a criminal."

"It was that dark stubble of a beard, a couple of days old, that cautioned me. I certainly didn't think you were the CEO of a big corporation." She winked, then sauntered into the hallway and waited for him to show her where the kitchen was.

Shane passed her in the corridor. "Anna and Kevin think you're a special friend visiting. The only person who knows who you really are is my head of security."

"Don't you think they'll wonder why I roam around the house in the middle of night, checking doors and windows?"

"They'll just have to wonder. I love both of them, and they've been with me for many years, but Anna can't keep a secret, and I'm afraid she'd let something slip, especially when my executive assistant is here tomorrow." He paused near a door, closed the space between them and leaned in to whisper, "If you roam the house in the middle of the night, when are you going to sleep?"

Her pulse rate spiked from his nearness, but she didn't step away. "That depends on your security system, which I need to see in this tour."

"I bring a woman home, and the first thing she looks at is my security system. What do you think Anna and Kevin will think then?"

Tess chuckled. "Tell them anything you want. Tell them I have this thing about staying in a house that doesn't have a good security system, that I feel better after I see how safe a place is."

He tossed back his head and laughed, a deep belly kind. "They'll think you're strange, and I'm just as strange for falling for you."

The sound of his merriment urged her to join in, but she had to focus on business, not pleasure. "I figure they already think you're strange, bringing a woman home right after your daughter leaves, especially one they haven't heard about."

He sobered. "They'll be tickled. Anna has been trying to get me to date again. She's taken me to task for working twenty-four/seven and was the one who was happy when I decided to go for the hike that led to this." He swept his hand toward his injured leg.

Suspicion pricked her. "She was? How long have she and Kevin been working for you?"

"Since I married Elena."

"How about your executive assistant?"

"Ten years."

"And Nick Compton?"

"Five years. He started right after he left the army."

"Interesting."

"I know that tone. You think one of them could be involved. I think I know the employees who work closely with me better than that. Next, you're going to ask about my daughter."

Her eyes widened at the fierceness in his voice. "I have to suspect everyone. You don't."

The door behind Shane opened, and a

petite woman no more than five feet tall with salt and pepper hair pulled in a tight bun at her nape fixed her gaze on them. "What's taking you so long to bring her in to meet me? You two have been out here for five minutes. I thought I raised you better than that, Shane."

"Raised you?" Tess murmured as she came around from behind Shane to greet the housekeeper.

"Yes, she was my nanny years ago, and later, I convinced her to come work for me. Anna, this is ... my lady friend, Tess Miller."

The way he said *lady friend* as though it were true made her face heat. Tess shook the older woman's hand. "He's been telling me all about you."

"That's good, because until this morning, I didn't know you existed." Anna eyed Tess as though the housekeeper was inspecting the vegetables at the market. "And just so you know, I'm not ancient. He has been responsible for my gray hairs. He was the first and only child I was ever a nanny for." She swung her attention to him. "And what happened to you this week put a few more gray hairs on my head." As she turned and disappeared into the room, she added, "Come in and have some tea with me before I start dinner."

"She rules the house, not me," he whispered.

"Really? I would never have known that. You can run along. I'll probably get your life history by the time I finish my tea."

"You're supposed to be guarding me, so that's best done by my side."

That declaration heightened the heat of her blush. She shouldn't have taken this job. Only a few more days until the merger went through, and then he could have two big burly bodyguards plastered to his sides.

"The tea is getting cold." Anna carried the tray with the cups and the teapot on it to the kitchen table.

Tess entered the kitchen with Shane slightly behind her, almost touching. He could be clear across the room, and she'd be aware of his location—even if she weren't his bodyguard.

"Just so you know, Anna loves to embellish some of my childhood."

"Thanks for the warning. This should be interesting." Tess turned a smile on Anna, intending to discover as much as she could about the man who piqued her interest far beyond the job.

* * *

Early the next morning, before anyone was up, Tess prowled the ground floor, checking doors and windows, more as something to do than thinking they might be unlocked. Shane's security system was excellent. He had said his head of security was responsible for making sure his house was protected. She would thank Neil Compton when she met him. He and Diane Flood, Shane's executive assistant, were coming out today.

Tess paused at the large window that overlooked the front of his estate. It had a high wall around it and a sturdy gate, requiring visitors to call the main house to be buzzed in. Although no place was totally secure, it would be easier to guard him at his home. If Shane never left until the merger was announced, he should be safe. In two days, though, he had to attend the big party at the VT's president's house. That might present a problem. She'd have to glue herself to Shane's side and pretend for a whole room full of people they were a couple while watching for someone to make a move against him.

"You're up early."

The husky voice of the man who'd haunted her dreams last night cut into her thoughts. She turned toward him, hidden in the shadows by the entrance into the living room. But she felt the intensity pouring off of him and the drill of his gaze. She sucked in a deep breath and held it for seconds longer than usual.

"Is everything okay? Did something disturb your sleep?" Shane moved into the muted glow of the lamplight. Dressed in jeans and a long sleeve navy blue pullover, he looked comfortable and casual in the midst of the elegant room. His hair was tousled, as if he'd finger-combed it, and he was barefooted.

"It's four. I got five hours of sleep.

That's all I need."

"That's about all I require, too."

Another thing they had in common. After her conversation with Anna yesterday, she'd learned she and Shane liked a lot of the same things: hiking, roughing it in the wilds, photography, coffee, pecan pie. She'd seen some of his photos as she'd toured the house and was impressed with how he could capture a scene at its essence. She'd recently taken up photography, because she traveled so much and saw some beautiful places. So she often took a couple of days to tour wherever she'd been working after her job was over.

Tess realized she'd been staring at Shane. What had he said? Oh, yeah. Sleep. "When I work, I sometimes sleep less," Tess finally said when she realized she was staring at him and a long silence had fallen between them. "I see your daughter likes to ride horses."

He came to her side. "Likes? Oh, no. *Love* is a better word. And at my parents' she'll get to ride a lot."

Tess shut the drapes and edged away

from the window, so Shane wasn't exposed. "I got that feeling when I saw all the riding trophies in her bedroom."

"Do you like to ride?"

"Love is a better word for me, too. Every time I go to Uncle Jack's, I ride a couple of times a day, often with my uncle. That's one of the things I miss the most when I'm working, so I probably overdo it when I'm back in Phoenix."

"I have a small stable where I keep four horses. We could—"

"As much as I'd love to, I'd rather you not leave this house until we have to." It wasn't just about his security. If they rode together, it would just give them another thing in common.

"You think someone is out there?"

"Could be."

"I'd never thought of my home being anything but a safe haven."

"That's what I thought about the cabin. A retreat for me."

One of his eyebrows arched. "But not now?"

"Nowhere is completely safe. It's hard

not to realize that in my line of work, but with the cabin, I put the outside world behind me. It was me, nature and sometimes Uncle Jack."

"And I ruined that for you." He reached out and touched her arm. "I'm sorry."

"I wouldn't have wanted it any other way. That's the only cabin around for several miles. You needed ..." She couldn't finish that. This job was more than just bodyguard and client. *Lord, what are You doing? I've never had this much trouble separating my professional and personal lives.*

"I know I needed you. I'm just lucky I didn't fall over a cliff to the valley below." He stepped closer and took her hand. "No words can express my gratitude to you and your uncle. My daughter has already lost her mother. I couldn't let her lose her dad, too. She took Elena's death so hard."

The sadness in his voice made her think about her mother. She knew how he felt.

His hands framed her face. "You okay? Have you lost someone close to you? You never talk about your parents. Just your uncle."

She needed to back away, but the look of concern in his eyes touched a chord deep inside her, strengthening a bond that had begun forming from the moment he stumbled into the cabin. "My mother killed herself. She drank too much and mixed alcohol with pills. I couldn't do anything to save her."

"Is that why you protect people now?"

Is it? "I was attacked in my home when I was sixteen. I think that's what really made me want to protect others. I couldn't defend myself. It took months to recover. That's when Uncle Jack insisted I come live with him and Patricia in New York. Then he started teaching me to defend myself."

"Where was your father when all this happened?"

She stiffened and pulled away from him. "Drunk."

SIX

That one word. *Drunk*. It was so full of suppressed anger, it hung in the air between them. Shane realized the physical wounds from Tess's attack had healed, but not the emotional ones, especially the feelings concerning her father.

He took her hand. "I need some coffee. Want some?"

She looked away but nodded. The hard line of her jaw attested to her battle for control. He wanted to know much more about her. The pain emanating from her pierced his heart and made him feel what she must have gone through. Since Elena's death, he'd thought his feelings had been suspended, locked away in a block of ice. But not now.

Their hands still clasped, Shane made his way into the foyer, then the hallway that led to the kitchen. He slanted a look toward Tess, and a tic jerked in her cheek. He wanted to say something to comfort her, but he was at a loss. The house was so quiet that he heard his heart pounding in his ears.

He flipped the overhead light on as he entered the room.

She disconnected their link and crossed her arms.

He headed for the counter and the pot, giving her time to compose herself while he prepared the coffee.

"Will we wake up Kevin and Anna?" Tess asked as she prowled the perimeter, trying the back door, glancing out the windows. She wouldn't be able to see much because of the bright lights in the kitchen.

He watched her moving restlessly, as if she were struggling with something. "Anna is used to me coming in here early and fix-ing coffee. After it perks, we can go into the den and drink it. I usually go to my home office and work."

At the bay window in the breakfast nook, Tess spun around. "Listen. About what I said ... I didn't mean to bring my personal life into this."

"I started it by telling you about Elena." He took down some mugs and filled them with hot, fragrant coffee, then handed her one. "Let's sit in the den."

A minute later when he settled on the couch next to her, he continued. "I didn't intend to tell you about Elena, either. It isn't something I share. My life was going along nicely, and then suddenly, everything changed. I felt as though I was put in a blender and the off button was missing. I kept going around and around."

"I know that feeling. I told Uncle Jack about the attack once. I've never discussed it again. I wanted to put it behind me and move forward."

"Did you?"

"I thought I had, but Uncle Jack keeps expecting me to forgive my dad. He thinks I need to do it to move on completely."

"Like I have to accept Elena is gone?"

"I suppose. I know God wants me to forgive him, but it's so hard. I was in the hospital for almost a day before the police found my dad, drunk and passed out in his car. As far as I was concerned, he shouldn't have come to visit me. He made me feel like the attack was my fault. He complained about having to clean up the mess at home and deal with the insurance company and the police."

"Did they ever find who did it?"

"Two young guys high on drugs, looking for money. I interrupted them, and they went crazy. Strangely, I've been able to forgive them. What they did led to me moving to New York to live with Uncle Jack. That changed my life for the better."

The urge to draw her into his embrace overwhelmed Shane, but he didn't want to stop her from talking. She needed to, just like he did. "What about your father?"

"The day I went to Uncle Jack's was the day he dismissed me from his life. My uncle says he's still drinking."

"Did he always drink?"

"No. He started after my mother committed suicide. I tried to get him to stop, but he just got angrier and meaner."

"Suicide is hard for the people left behind." The thought of what Tess went through contracted his chest, and he inhaled a deep breath then slowly released it.

Her eyes glistened, and she swallowed hard. "I know. I was twelve. She got hooked on pain meds." Tess stared down at her lap, cradling the mug in her hands. "I don't think she meant to kill herself, but she began mixing alcohol and her pills, and one day, she didn't wake up. I didn't understand at the time."

"Maybe your dad blames himself and couldn't deal with the guilt."

She glanced at Shane. "So you think I should forgive him, too." Her words held a hard edge.

"I can't tell you what you need to do, but I do think your uncle is a smart man." Shane took a long sip of his coffee.

"I shouldn't have left you alone with Uncle Jack." She studied the dark liquid in her mug. "I'm surprised he didn't tell you my life story. He can be nosey. Must be the detective in him." She grumbled, but a smile flirted with the corners of her mouth.

"My childhood was pretty normal and uneventful. When Elena died unexpectedly, it really knocked my legs out from under me. If I hadn't had Rachel and the Lord, I might have gone down that path. There were times I wanted to escape the pain any way I could."

"I know what you mean. If it wasn't for the Lord, I'm not sure how I would have made it. My dad didn't believe in God, and I wasn't enough for him. Uncle Jack is the one who taught me about God's love. Uncle Jack is so different from my father."

"We are the sum of our experiences. After this is over, you can bet I will be looking at things differently. I have always realized having money could put a target on my back, but whoever is after me isn't doing it for a ransom. The second attempt proved that."

"Speaking of that, besides the party tomorrow night, will you need to leave here before you make your announcement about the merger?"

"No. Diane and Nick are coming here today, and Diane will come over tomorrow. We're making arrangements for the announcement, assuming the deal goes through. I'll meet with the board the day after the party, and a decision will be made then."

"What's the party for?" Tess swallowed a sip of coffee.

"To persuade a few who are against the merger. The vote may be close. From what the president of Virtual Technologies, Dale Mason, said yesterday there are two men who don't want this, and they're trying to influence the rest of the board members."

"Could they be behind the attempts on your life?"

"I've done several mergers over the past few years. I've had a couple that met opposition, but no one ever resorted to trying to kill me."

"Who are the men? I have told my boss about Anthony Revell, Mark Collins and Chase Temple. She's running a background check on them. I think I should have her run one on the men opposing the merger."

"Ben Smith. Together with Chase Temple, they own thirty-eight percent of the company."

"I like to know what I can about who might be behind the attempts on your life, but also have a photo of what they look like. All the information I can gather helps me be prepared while guarding you."

"In the latest development, Anthony Revell is making a play for Virtual Technologies. I won't be surprised if he's at the party. Should be an interesting evening."

"That depends on how you look at it. For me, I'd rather you passed on the party. It exposes you to whoever is after you."

"VT needs an infusion of money, whether it comes from my company or Revell's. I have my supporters on the board, and Revell has his." Just thinking about tomorrow evening made his neck muscles tighten like fists. The pain spread out from there. "Mark Collins was invited and probably will show up, too, although he hasn't made a formal move to merge with VT. There are one or two swing votes, which could shift everything toward Revell or even Collins. That's why I can't let the board know about the threats to my life."

"Then you think it will be over in a few days, and I can return to Dallas?"

"Yes." He wouldn't see Tess again, and he realized in that moment that he was bothered by that fact. He wanted to get to know her. He hadn't felt that way about a woman since he dated Elena. That surge of emotion—that surprised him.

"Are you okay?"

Tess's voice penetrated his stunned mind. He'd never considered becoming involved with another woman. To him, Elena had been his one true love.

"Shane?"

He blinked and focused on Tess's beautiful face, the one he saw when he'd first opened his eyes at the cabin. "There's nothing wrong."

"You paled. I thought you might have remembered something."

Yes, the way you looked when I recovered consciousness. Like an angel—my guardian angel. "I hope you'll give me

DEADLY HUNT

some time to hire another bodyguard."

"Of course, but you might contact my agency and talk with your head of security when he comes out today. I can give you some suggestions, if you want."

"Are you sure you won't stay?"

Her mouth twisted in a thoughtful look, and he waited, filled with hope.

"I really shouldn't. If you're going back and forth to work, you'll need more than one person. You might need to look at a full detail."

"You could be part of that."

She sighed, peered away for a long moment, and then met his gaze. "No. We need to stick to the agreement we made yesterday." She rose. "I'm going to refill my cup then continue my walk through the house."

Shane watched her leave, thinking about the wall that had gone up when he'd suggested she stay and guard him. Her professional façade, as he'd come to think of that persona, was firmly in place now. For a while, she'd let down her guard and been herself. He'd glimpsed the true wom-

127

an behind the front she presented to others.

As he finished the last of his coffee, he decided he needed to stop these thoughts about more with Tess. Her life wasn't suited to a relationship. Even if she weren't protecting him, she must travel all over the world, guarding others. These feelings developing for her were momentarily spurred by the fact she'd saved his life twice. Nothing more.

* * *

Shane sat at the dining room table with his work spread out as Diane Flood and he went through the business that needed to be done. Tess watched him from the living room across the foyer. His executive assistant hadn't questioned working at his house, but Tess had seen a puzzled look in her eyes when Diane had walked into the house. Shane and Diane, though, soon fell into a work pattern that included Shane taking occasional breaks to check on her. Tess was pretending to read a book on her electronic device a good part of the morning while perched in a rather uncomfortable wingback. Shane had even moved the large round table in the entry hall so she could see him. She checked her emails frequently, as her employer sent updated information on the men she was investigating. On the surface, all four men appeared to be upstanding members of the community, which didn't really mean anything. But at least Tess had their photos and now knew what they looked like.

At noon instead of eating the meal Anna had prepared, Diane left to run some errands for Shane. Nick, the head of security at DDI, arrived to join her and Shane for lunch at the game table in the den. Tess's stomach rumbled at the delicious scent of a Mexican casserole. After last night's dinner and this morning's breakfast, she couldn't wait to eat something else cooked by Anna. Definitely a perk of the job.

"Everything set up for the party tomorrow night?" Shane asked Nick as his security chief took his seat across from Tess.

"Yes. Dale Mason's staff has everything

covered. I and a few of my top men will be at the party. I'm the only one who knows about the threats, per your instructions, but they know keeping an eye on you is their priority."

"Good. Tess, do you have any concerns or questions?" Shane asked as he picked up his fork.

"I would like photos of each DDI security man at the party, as well as a diagram of where the party is taking place."

"I'll have them to you by the end of the day so you can familiarize yourself with the layout. I understand from Shane you've been a bodyguard for seven years."

Although not a question, Tess said, "It gives me an opportunity to see the world. I always wanted to travel."

Shane's forehead crinkled, and he lowered his head while he forked some of the Mexican casserole and ate it.

For the next ten minutes, Shane and Nick discussed a few issues at the corporation's headquarters in Phoenix. Tess heard the words, but they didn't really register. Instead she watched each one, cataloguing their mannerisms. She learned so much by studying a person's body language. Shane talked with his hands while Nick's movements were controlled and reserved.

When something bothered Shane, he would rub his nape while keeping his expression neutral. Some people might notice the look on his face at best, but most concentrated on what was said, not how it was spoken.

By the time the lunch was over, Tess was convinced she could trust Nick. He was a no-nonsense man who knew his job. But what had intrigued her most today was how Shane worked with his staff. He treated them as associates with valuable input. He respected his employees' opinions and let them know it. Much like her employer at the agency.

Shane and Nick relaxed back in their chairs and discussed the upcoming Phoenix Suns' season. Tess's mind was elsewhere, though, remembering the conversation she and Shane had shared in this room in the wee hours of the morning. She still couldn't believe she'd told Shane about her mother and father. She'd finally discussed the kind of childhood she'd had before going to live with her uncle and his wife. She'd held it inside so long, it felt good to share with Shane.

All morning while staring at the ebook she was supposed to be reading, she'd thought about what Shane had said about forgiving her father. She didn't know if she could. Even today, she felt the sting of her dad's words and the consequences of his drinking problem. Those things had affected every aspect of her life. How could she forgive that?

One step at a time.

The words flowed through her mind as though the Lord had spoken them directly to her. Was that possible? Could she let the hurt and anger go enough to forgive her father and move on?

Nick stood and turned toward Tess. "I'll be back by the end of the day with the information you need. I hope you can give us some good suggestions for a couple of bodyguards to replace you when we make the merger announcement."

Shane rose. "I tried to get her to recon-sider. She promised to stay until we find some good replacements."

Nick smiled. "Good." With a nod, he headed toward the foyer.

Shane came behind Tess's chair and pulled it out for her, leaning down to say, "I'll double your pay if you stay."

How could she? He knew more about her than most people, and that was only after a few days. She was managing to keep herself professionally focused, but she didn't know how long she could maintain that. She was beginning to care about him, and if it went any further, it might distract her from her work.

She pushed to her feet and turned, keeping the chair between them. "I haven't had a man pull a chair out for me in ages."

"You're just not hanging around with the right guys. Stay, and I'll pull your chair out all the time."

She started for the hallway. "I'm at a particularly fascinating part of the book I'm reading. I can't wait to get back to it."

Shane chuckled. "What's it about? Maybe I should read it."

"It's a romance. Nothing you would like."

"Try me."

"A woman meets a man, and they fall in love." She hurried her step.

He kept pace with her. "Interesting you like to read romances."

She halted in the foyer and faced him. "What's that mean?"

"I would have pegged you for a thriller reader."

"Too close to my job. I prefer a change of pace."

Nick stood in the entrance talking with Diane who carried a big white box. Nick glanced at Shane and Tess, said something else to Diane, then left.

Tess nodded to Shane's executive assistant. "I'll leave you to your work." She headed for the living room.

But Shane clasped her arm. "Wait. She went to pick up something for you."

The feel of his fingers sent her heartbeat racing. She needed space. She needed to leave before he had her whole life history. And her heart. Two, three at the most, days left. *I can do this.*

"It's in the white box?" Tess eyed Diane as she and Shane covered the distance to the woman.

"Yes." Then to Diane, Shane said, "Thanks for picking this up. I'll be in the dining room soon."

His executive assistant handed him the box, gave Tess a quick once-over, and walked away.

"C'mon. I want to see you open it." Shane placed his hand on the small of her back and started for the living room.

Heat seared Tess's face. The only person she exchanged gifts with was Uncle Jack.

Shane presented her with the box. "Open it."

When she did, her eyes widened on a beautiful, emerald green cocktail dress nestled in the white tissue paper. "I can't accept this." She looked up. "Why did you buy me this?"

"For tomorrow night. Surely, you didn't already have a dress in that duffel bag you brought with you."

"But I was going to wear..." What? Had she really thought that black slacks and a white blouse would be appropriate for a fancy cocktail party? "Frankly, I didn't think about what I was going to wear, and you're right. I didn't bring anything appropriate." This was what he did to her—flustered her to the point she didn't think of every contingency.

She lifted the dress out of the box and checked its size. Six. How did he know?

"And I had Diane pick up some shoes and a purse to match. If something doesn't fit, she can take it back and get the right size. Go try it on." A smile spread across his mouth.

"I'll try the dress on later, but I'll see if the shoes fit." Tess sat in a chair and slipped on the matching emerald green two-inch heels. She felt like Cinderella with Prince Charming standing in front of her, waiting to see if she was the one he'd danced with at the ball. "They fit."

"And this purse is plenty big enough for your gun." He held the evening bag up, his smile infectious.

She couldn't resist grinning back at Shane. "Thank you. Now I'll fit in at the"—she almost said ball—"cocktail party."

He set the box on the couch nearby. "Well, I'd better go work."

As he left, Tess murmured, "Thank you. I love it."

He glanced over his shoulder. "It's perfect for you."

His intense look caused butterflies to flutter in her stomach.

Only a few more days. Why aren't I happier about that?

* * *

Tess put the finishing touches to her make-up, which she rarely wore. Then she stepped back to check her reflection in the full-length mirror. Diane had told her that Shane had personally picked the cocktail dress out for her, using a Phoenix high-end store that had a large online presence. Tess couldn't believe how well it fit her. Its shimmering satin fell in soft folds below her knees.

This wasn't her first time to dress up on the job, but as she turned from side to side, she felt like Cinderella again. Like yesterday when he presented her with the dress, she realized how emotionally invested she was becoming with Shane. It scared her. What if something happened to him? She would blame herself, always wondering if she'd blown it because she was becoming more focused on him instead of the job.

"Show time," she whispered to her image in the mirror.

She snatched up her purse and snapped it open to check her weapon inside. It was loaded and ready. She wouldn't let Shane down. He was her only concern tonight. Soon this assignment would be over, and she could get back to her normal life.

Shane waited for her at the bottom of the staircase. As she descended the steps, he moved forward, hardly limping, and watched her. The sight of him in his black tuxedo, so different from the day she'd met him, stole her breath. She had to force herself to breathe.

"You clean up nicely." A smile flirted with the corners of her mouth as if he were her date to the senior prom. She stopped on the first step.

His gray eyes lit like polished silver. "I could say the same for you, but it wouldn't be an adequate description." One of his hands cupped her face.

Standing on the bottom step, still having to look up slightly into his gaze, she needed to end the warm touch of his palm against her cheek, but she felt paralyzed by the mesmerizing expression in those gray depths. For a few seconds while he bent his head toward hers, she forgot she was his bodyguard. He made her feel special, as though she were the only woman in his life. The anticipation of his lips brushing against hers spurred her heartbeat. She swayed toward him.

SEVEN

Shane wrapped his arms around Tess, tugging her until she pressed against him. His mouth came down to claim hers completely. He hadn't kissed a woman since Elena, and the sensations Tess created in him rocked him to his core. Suddenly, he didn't want to go to the party. He wanted to spend the evening alone with Tess, getting to know her even better. Her embrace enveloped him, and he imagined their hearts beating as one.

Someone cleared a throat. The sound irritated him, and he wanted whoever was in the foyer with them to leave, but reality intruded. Tess pulled away. She straightened and stepped to the side as if nothing had happened between them. Only the flush of her cheeks remained to indicate she'd enjoyed the kiss as much as he had.

He didn't want her to leave after the decision on the merger was announced, but Nick had told him today he'd found two excellent bodyguards who could take over as soon as he was ready. He'd been working on this merger for almost a year, and now he wished he could delay the decision a few more days.

Turning slowly, he composed himself and faced his head of security, who was their driver to the party. "You're right on time. We're ready. Let's get this over with."

He offered Tess his arm and escorted her to the double front doors. He saw the puzzled look Nick had tossed at him and thought about saying he was preparing for his role as Tess's date. Nick knew him better than that.

When Shane settled into the back of the limousine, he slid a glance toward Tess who had slipped into her bodyguard mode— alert, assessing her environment, focused on her job. He should be happy about that. One part of him was, but another part wished this was a normal date and that he and Tess could enjoy the evening as a true couple.

She shifted toward him, her purse in her lap with her hand covering her bag. He studied her expression in the soft lighting. It revealed nothing of what she was thinking. Not anything like when she'd been on the staircase. He released a long breath.

"In a few hours this will be over," she said, all business now. "I'll be right beside you the whole evening. I'm not going to let anything happen to you."

Although her tone was businesslike, there was a hint of something beneath her words. Concern? Regret? "I know. But you'll have to relax and play the part of my date."

"Don't worry. I will."

* * *

An hour later on the edge of a small ballroom, Tess watched the crowd and Shane.

It reminded her of a jammed marketplace she'd visited in Spain where her client was nearly kidnapped. Too many people, too much noise. And while being vigilant about her surroundings, she had to act like she was in love with Shane. Truth was, that last part wasn't that difficult. Watching Shane was easy. Tearing her eyes away to focus on the crowd—that was the hard part. But Shane's life was in the balance, and she wouldn't risk him by giving into the feelings churning her stomach.

Lord, help me do what needs to be done.

Shane leaned toward her ear and whispered, "Here comes Dale Mason, the president, and Chase Temple, one of the board members who doesn't want to merge with DDI."

She'd memorized the looks of the main players in this merger. She'd already seen and met Mark Collins. Anthony Revell was across the room, occasionally throwing a glance Shane's way. No love lost there.

"I haven't seen Ben Smith yet," he continued. "Surely he'll be here."

Tess curled her arm around Shane and pressed close to him as if she were enthralled with every word he said. She was playing her part.

Not true. I am enthralled, and that's the problem.

"Ah, I see Ben in the entrance with his wife," Shane said.

Chase and Dale stopped in front of them, and Shane smiled at them. Tess was impressed at how well he carried his façade. Most people couldn't smile at a man they suspected might've been trying to kill them.

Chase Temple was a large man, built like a linebacker, and he blocked Tess's view of the rest of the guests.

A frown marred the president of Virtual Technologies' face. "We need to talk to you." He looked at Tess, then back at Shane. "In *private*. Something has come to our attention."

When Shane stiffened, Tess squeezed his arm then slipped her hand away. "I can leave you three alone right now." Then she leaned close and whispered, "I won't be far away, keeping my eye on you."

Shane turned partly away from the two gentlemen and gave Tess a quick kiss on her cheek near her ear. "Dale is the one person on DDI's side."

Before she moved away, Dale Mason said, "We'll go into my library, Shane. I don't want anyone overhearing us."

Shane threw her a glance then smiled at the two men. Tess could tell it was forced, because his eyes didn't light up as they usually did when he genuinely grinned.

"Gentlemen, I'm at your disposal."

Tess forged her way through the fifty guests toward the entrance, so she could watch which room the trio entered. The layout of the house Nick had given her indicated a study, but not a library. Were they the same room?

Near the doorway into the corridor, Chase said something to Shane and Dale, then excused himself and made his way toward Ben Smith about ten feet off to the side. Strange. With the absence of Chase, Tess relaxed a little. She exited the ballroom and hurried across the hall, where she entered the powder room. She immediately spun around and cracked the door open to watch the president and Shane head down the hallway. When they disappeared, around the corner, she came out of the restroom and quickened her step after the pair. She rounded the corner as a door closed at the end of the corridor.

Nick came up behind her. "I saw you take off. What's happening?"

"Shane went with Dale Mason. The man wants to talk with him about a concern. My first impulse is to barge into the room, but that wouldn't put Dale's mind at peace. I wonder what he'd think if he found me standing guard in the hallway."

"I've got an idea. We could be talking right here." He stepped across from her and propped his shoulder against the wall on the other side. "Now you can keep an eye on the door. There's only one way into that room. Shane will be safe with Dale."

"What do you want to talk about? The weather?"

Nick smiled. "It's been perfect the last

few days. Not too hot."

Tess chuckled. "What did you do before this?"

"I was in the military."

"I noticed you wear a wedding ring. Tell me about your wife."

"She's the love of my life."

As he said it, the shadow in his eyes didn't coincide with his words. She wondered if they were having marital problems. According to Shane, Nick kept long hours at DDI. Tess started to say something when the door opened and Shane and Mr. Mason came out. Shane's smile reached deep into his eyes, and Tess's tensed shoulders sagged.

"It looks like they cleared it up," she murmured to Nick. She stepped toward the pair coming down the hall. "I hope the business portion of the evening is over with, darling." With what she hoped was an adoring look, she approached Shane and fell into step next to him.

"Yes, Dale and I have come to agreement, and it should become official tomorrow after the board meeting."

"It was nice meeting you, Ms. Miller. You do a good job watching over Shane." Mr. Mason shook Tess's hand. "If you all will excuse me, I'd better get back to my guests." He nodded toward Shane and Nick before he sauntered toward the ballroom.

"Nick, we're leaving. There's no reason for us to stay, and I'm sure Tess would prefer if I were at home rather than out in the open."

"I'll bring the car around."

As Nick left, Shane faced her. "Chase Temple informed Dale that the hunting accident was really an attempt on my life."

"How did he find out?"

"Anthony Revell told Chase, who immediately ran to Dale and everyone else on the board he could find."

"Mr. Mason didn't seem to be concerned about it."

"I assured him that my corporation is his best bet to revive his own, whether I was at the head or not. I also told him I have taken precautions. Our two companies will make a powerful team."

"You told him about me?"

Shane nodded. "As well as what security measures would be put in place when the merger was announced. I'm not taking the threats to my life lightly."

"This is one ... bodyguard who is glad you aren't. You're right. I'll feel better when we're back at your house."

When the limousine pulled up to the door, Tess exited the house first and scanned her surroundings before giving Shane the signal to follow. The valet opened the car door, and Shane and Tess slid into the luxurious car. The limo pulled away from the entrance.

Shane took her hand. "I'm glad that's over with. I hate working a party, and I can imagine you were bored."

"No, not bored. I was too busy watching all the people, hoping we could leave when you persuaded that board member to vote for DDI tomorrow. From what you said, that would cinch your merger."

"I'm glad I stayed around. I knew Chase Temple wasn't in favor of my company merging with Virtual Technologies, but I didn't know exactly who he wanted, because the corporation needed an influx of money. Now I believe he's working with Anthony Revell."

In two days she'd be gone, and none of this would be her problem, but she wished the person behind the attempts on Shane's life would be caught before she left Phoenix.

"We need to talk about what happened on the staircase, Tess. You can't deny there are feelings between us."

She closed her eyes for a few seconds and fortified herself with a deep inhalation, then let it go slowly. "We live in two different worlds. When I stop long enough to be home, I live in Dallas. I don't think it's a good idea for ..." Her words came to a halt as the limousine did at an intersection.

Nick turned to face them. The locks clicked, and the door next to Shane flew open. Tess had her hand in her purse when Nick pointed a weapon at her.

"Don't even think about it." Shane's head of security's voice was lethally quiet. "Give your purse to my associate."

The man in the doorway had a revolver

aimed at Shane's chest. Reluctantly, Tess handed him her purse while noting two things about the man: the scent of tobacco emanating from him and a white bandage around his forearm. One of the men in the ditch?

"Good girl," Nick said.

The man in the doorway set her purse on top of the limo, never taking his gaze off of them. A moment later, he yanked a pair of handcuffs from his back pocket.

Nick spoke again. "Shane, take the handcuffs and put them on Tess, arms behind her back."

The soft interior light cast a shadow across Nick's face, but Tess spied the fierce determination in his eyes and shivered. "So Nick, was that you shooting at us that day when Shane came to my uncle's ranch?"

"Yes. I didn't think he'd convince you to guard him." Nick returned his attention to Shane. "Now lean forward. Your turn to be handcuffed. I don't want you two to run away before I get the ransom."

"The ransom?" Shane asked.

"My friend here will be taking you two

away, leaving me beside the road for dead. He'll knock me out and shoot me in the chest, not realizing that I have a bullet proof vest, like any security guy would wear when there has been a threat against the employer he's protecting."

"What do you think that will accomplish?" Shane asked. "You know I've made arrangements that no ransom can be paid for my kidnapping from company funds."

"Maybe not, but I bet your parents won't let their only granddaughter be without her father. I'll make sure of that when I talk with them tomorrow."

"Why are you doing this?" Shane bit out the last word between clenched teeth.

"Money, of course."

While Shane occupied Nick's attention, Tess slowly worked her hands down behind the back of the seat. Thank God she'd hidden her second weapon there earlier. She also had a knife strapped to her thigh, but with her hands behind her back, that would be harder to get.

"Don't do this, Nick," Shane said, a nerve jerking in his jaw line.

"Too late. I was committed when Mark Collins approached me about taking you out. With his money and your parents' money, I can get lost and live the kind of life I should've."

"What about your wife?" Tess asked as she worked the handle of the gun into her right palm.

"She walked out on me three months ago. I have nothing to lose. I'm gonna start over in a place the authorities will never find me, assuming they even figure out I'm behind it. Let's go, Cal. You know what to do."

After Cal shut the door and the locks clicked closed, Nick left the front seat and rounded the rear of the limousine.

"Keep an eye on them, I stashed a gun in here earlier." Tess had to get her cuffed hands around to the front.

"Cal hit Nick," Shane said, his voice not betraying any emotion. "He went down."

The sound of the gunshot shuddered down Tess's spine as she brought her arms under her backside and wiggled her legs through the tight loop formed by her bound hands. "It's a good thing I have long arms, or this wouldn't work."

"Cal's coming around to the driver's side."

Tess stopped moving and buried her hands in the folds of her dress, praying the thug didn't look back at them until he got into the limousine. "Good thing Nick left the glass partition open. It gives me a good shot when Cal gets in."

Right on cue, the assailant unlocked the driver's door and opened it. The interior lights popped on. As the man climbed in, he turned toward them. Tess raised her gun and leveled it at the man's head.

"I'm an expert shot, and before you get your weapon up, you'll have a bullet in your brain."

The thug paled.

"Lift your gun up slowly by the barrel then drop it on the backseat floor. I won't hesitate to kill you if you try anything." A steel thread wove through her voice with the last sentence emphasized.

Cal did as instructed.

"Now toss me the key to the handcuffs.

I will be watching."

While she talked, Shane contorted himself until his hands were in front of him, too. A few grunts peppered the air, but Tess didn't take her eyes off Cal. When he threw the key into the back, Shane caught it with his bound hands and began working on his lock. Freed, he took Cal's weapon from the floor and aimed it at him.

"Unlock your cuffs, Tess. I've got him." He turned his attention to Cal. "And just so you know, I know how to use this weapon."

Tess hurried to free herself. "Unlock the back doors."

When she heard the click, she slipped out. "I'll be greeting Nick when he awakens. Hand me your cell. I'll call the police."

Standing behind the limousine watching Nick slowly wake up, Tess placed a 911 call then waited. It was over, all except rounding up Mark Collins.

* * *

The next day after the police left, Tess finally allowed herself to relax. She and

155

Shane were sitting in his den. He'd been on the phone a number of times that morning, but she'd stayed in her comfortable place. Her job was over. Mark Collins had been arrested, along with Nick and Cal. Seemed they'd planned for the suspicion to fall on Anthony Revell. Shane was the driving force behind DDI, and with him gone, Mark planned to offer Virtual Technologies a merger that would make them competitive with what was left of Shane's company for the majority share of the marketplace. It was unthinkable the things people would do for money.

Her packed duffel bag was in Uncle Jack's Jeep, and she would leave as soon as Shane heard if the Virtual Technologies' board approved the merger. He'd been on the phone an hour earlier talking with Dale Mason about what had happened. She'd heard his voice as they'd spoken about the new prospects for both companies as they blended their technology together. Listening to Shane's excitement made her wish she felt that way about her work. Never before had she been dissatisfied with her job.

Where had these feelings come from? And why? Because her vacation had been disrupted? It didn't matter. When she returned to Dallas and her life, she'd be fine.

The phone rang, and Shane snatched up the receiver. A smile transformed his whole bearing. When he hung up, he said, "It's official. We're merging with Virtual Technologies."

"I'm glad it worked out. I'm not surprised, though. They'd be foolish to work with anyone but you."

That was her cue. It was time to go.

"The new gaming system they're developing will be fantastic, and with our capabilities, we'll be unstoppable." He rounded his desk and came toward her. "A week ago, I didn't know if I'd see this happen. It wasn't that long ago I was in Jack's cabin, fighting for my life."

Tess stood. "Speaking about your life, I need to get back to mine." She straightened her clothes and pushed back her shoulders, pushing away her feelings for him at the same time. Those feelings should never have developed in the first place. His world was so different from hers.

He bridged the few feet between them and took her hands. "Can't you stay a while and finally have the vacation I interrupted?"

"No, I need to get back to Dallas." *Then I can start forgetting you*.

"Why? You have an apartment there you stay in only because of your job." He tugged her nearer, wrapping his arms around her. "I want us to get to know each other even better."

She felt as though she already knew Shane better than a lot of people. She'd seen him in tough situations, the kinds of situations that could bring out both the best and the worst in people. She loved what she'd discovered—his best. But this ... this falling in love thing? This lifestyle? It wasn't her. She relished living simply, relying only on herself. Having servants didn't fit her lifestyle. Neither did having a man in her life.

"I have to make a living. My job isn't here."

"What if I offered you Nick's position? I

need a new head of security, and I've seen you at work. Nothing gets past you."

She stepped away, breaking his embrace. "No. Uncle Jack would be better suited to that job. Ask him."

"What are you afraid of? Remember the kiss on the staircase? I want to see where it leads."

It leads to heartache. She remembered her parents' marriage. Uncle Jack's was good, but most weren't like his. And even his led to heartache. "That kiss should never have happened. You're mistaking gratitude for something more. We both need to forget the kiss and move on. I'm leaving." She pivoted and marched toward the front door, berating herself for ever letting down her professional guard and getting close to Shane.

As she drove toward Uncle Jack's ranch, she made plans to be on a plane for Dallas first thing in the morning. His daughter would be coming back home, and before long, Shane's life would return to normal. And so would hers.

* * *

Shane stared at the closed door a long moment after Tess left. His chest constricted him, making breathing difficult. *Forget the kiss*. He didn't know if he could. He'd felt as if he'd come home in her arms. Raking his hand through his hair, he began pacing, his thoughts racing.

Maybe she was right. What had transpired between them was all built on the fact that she'd saved his life. He was grateful, not falling in love. If that were the case, once he threw himself into his work he'd forget her.

EIGHT

Three months later

Tess was in her tiny living room in the middle of her exercise routine when her cell phone rang. She wanted to ignore it, but what if it was her boss calling with a new assignment? Her last one had ended a few days ago, and she was ready for another job. Anything to keep herself from thinking about Shane.

She grabbed her cell phone off the coffee table and frowned when she saw the number. She almost didn't answer. But she'd made the first move, writing him a letter. Seemed wrong to ignore him now.

Her finger hovered over the button as she fought her fear. She'd finally forgiven him for the past and had told him that in her letter. She hadn't been able to bring herself to call him and say the words, although she'd meant them. Bitterness and anger that she'd been carrying had only pulled her down and hurt her. Shane and her uncle had been right about forgiveness.

She punched the answer button. "Hello."

"I didn't do anything wrong. I don't need your *forgiveness*." Her father spat the word. "Your mother killed herself. That wasn't my fault. And you wanted to leave me. I didn't send you away."

For a few seconds her dad's raspy voice chilled her as if he were right in front of her, belittling her for something she'd done. Then she thought of God and the peace she'd experienced when she'd written the letter last week. She wouldn't let her father rob her of that peace anymore.

"I'm sorry you feel that way, but it doesn't change how I feel. I forgive you for what happened all those years ago. I wish

you the best. Please take care of yourself."
And I really mean that.

"How ... dare ...?" His words sputtered
to a stop.

Dead silence followed.

"Good bye, Dad."

The sound of his phone slamming filled
her ear before she had a chance to discon-
nect her cell phone. She bowed her head
and said, "Please, Lord, help him. He's in
Your hands."

When she began her next exercise, she
lost herself in it, clearing her mind.

Until five minutes later when the doorbell interrupted her.

Grasping a hand towel, she wiped her
sweaty face and neck as she headed toward the door. Through the peephole, she
checked to see whom her visitor was.

Shane.

She rested her forehead against the
cool wood. What was he doing here? She'd
managed today only to think about him
once, so far. Of course, she'd only been
awake for two hours. No matter what she
did, even work, she couldn't get him out of

her mind.

And why did she have to be hot and sweaty. What timing! She looked at the ceiling. *Really, if this is Your idea of a joke, I don't think it's very funny.* But then she couldn't deny that rush of feelings. Shane. Here.

She looked through the peephole again and saw Shane start to walk away. She needed to let him go. But before she could stop herself, she unlocked her door and opened it.

He stopped and slowly turned around. His smile melted her insides. She clutched the doorjamb before her legs gave out. She'd missed him so much. Her dreams every night hadn't done him justice.

"Why are you here?" she finally asked. "Uncle Jack would have told me if someone else was after you." Her uncle was working temporarily for Shane until he found the perfect head of security. Uncle Jack didn't want to work full-time, but he didn't mind helping Shane out for a short time.

"May I come in?"

She stepped to the side and allowed

him into her apartment, glad her roommate was gone. She didn't want to explain Shane to her. "I was exercising. I'd change, but I haven't finished yet." She was babbling. What she really wanted to do was throw her arms around his neck and kiss him.

"I've tried to stay away, but I can't do it any longer. Ever since you've left, all I think about is you. Instead of time making it better, it's getting worse with you gone. Please reconsider moving to Phoenix. If you don't want to be the head of security at DDI, then work from Phoenix. Jack tells me you really don't have to be in the same town as your agency."

"My uncle has a big mouth."

"Is it true?"

"Yes. But us working together probably wouldn't be a good idea. My parents did, and it was disastrous."

"We aren't your parents. You can still be a bodyguard. You can do whatever you want to do. I don't care. I just know I want you in my life. I love you, Tess."

His declaration zapped her as if she'd held a live electrical wire and survived the shock. "But we were only together a week." She could hardly contain the urge to hold him, but she had to be sensible.

"A very intense week. We skipped the casual dating part of a relationship."

She nodded slowly. "Our feelings are probably not based on anything normal for a couple."

His eyebrows lifted. "*Our* feelings?"

She shrugged, heat filling her face.

"So what if we started differently than other couples? What's wrong with that? I never thought of myself as *normal* anyway. Tell me one thing. How do you feel about me?"

Her throat tightened, locking inside the words she'd wanted to tell him so many times over the past few months.

His earnest expression fell.

"I care about you." No, no. She couldn't lie to him. "That's not quite all. I guess ... you're always in my thoughts. I've gone over our short time together so many times, trying to understand. A relationship takes months, years to develop. How can I feel like this after just a week?"

"Like ... this?" he prompted.

"How can I have fallen in love so quick-ly?"

He gathered her into his arms. "I don't know, and I don't care how we got here. The important part is how we feel. Please, give us a chance. Come to Phoenix. We can become a normal couple and date for months if you want."

She buried her face into his chest, sud-denly dying to confess everything. "Can I tell you one of the dreams I had? I dreamed I was having your baby. A child. Me. I mean, I love kids, but I never thought ..."

He cupped her face. "I think that's a beautiful dream. I know my daughter would love to have a little brother or sister."

"But I haven't even met Rachel."

"That's easy to remedy. Come back to Phoenix with me. Stay at my house or at your uncle's. Whatever you want, but just give us a chance. You can continue to work as a bodyguard or at DDI in security. Or" — he brushed his lips across hers— "you can marry me and have that baby you dreamed about."

It was sweet that he gave her the option to keep working, but she couldn't imagine keeping her job. How could she go on
all those trips away when she had him at
home, waiting for her?

"Okay. If we promise to take it slow. I
want to get to know Rachel. Mostly, I want
to be with you." Locking her arms around
him, she stood on her tiptoes and kissed
him with all her love. Here in his embrace,
this was where she belonged.

Dear Reader,

Thank you for reading *Deadly Hunt*, the first book in the **Strong Women, Extraordinary Situations Series**. The second book in the series is *Deadly Intent*. The third book is *Deadly Holiday*, highlighting another strong woman (a single mom and teacher) faced with dangerous circumstances. The fourth is *Deadly Countdown*, and the fifth is *Deadly Noel*.

Margaret Daley

Check out other books by Margaret Daley at http://margaretdaley.com/all-books/

DEADLY INTENT

Book 2 in
Strong Women, Extraordinary Situations
by Margaret Daley

Texas Ranger Sarah Osborn thought she would never see her high school sweetheart, Ian O'Leary, again. But fifteen years later, Ian, an ex-FBI agent, has someone targeting him, and she's assigned to the case. Can Sarah protect Ian and her heart?

Excerpt from
DEADLY INTENT
Book 2

Texas Ranger Sarah Osborn approached the man at the paddock. He faced away from her, his arms resting on the top slat of the fence. His tall, lean build radiated tension as he fisted his hands. She could see his biceps flexing beneath the T-shirt. There'd been a time she knew Ian O'Leary well. But not anymore. Maybe never.

"Ian," she called out. "I'm here about your stolen stallion."

He stiffened, pushed away from the wooden railing, and swung around. The tan cowboy hat shadowed his expression, but there was no mistaking his anger—the hard line of his jaw gave that away. "I heard you were assigned to this area, but I'd expected the sheriff. What's a Ranger doing investigating a stolen horse?"

"I'm heading a multi-county investigation into the recent cattle rustling."

"My prize stallion was taken. I don't have many cattle on this ranch, but the ones I have are accounted for."

"Sheriff Denison and I thought since a few horses have been taken, too, that this is the work of the same cattle rustlers." She didn't have to see his dark blue eyes to know they were drilling into her.

"Very well. What do you need from me?" A tic twitched in his cheek.

"To tell me what happened."

"I went through this with the sheriff this morning on the phone."

"Humor me. Run through it again." She ground her teeth to keep from saying what was really on her mind: Why did you come home? Since she worked several counties in this part of northeastern Texas, she'd managed for the past six months to keep her distance, but she couldn't avoid him forever.

2

He turned to the fence and gestured with his hand. "I keep Thunder near the barn. This is his paddock."

"When did you notice him gone?"

"About six this morning. I walk by here a bunch of times every day, since my home is so close."

As she walked toward the fence, she glanced over her shoulders at the simple red brick, one-story house with a long front porch, and if she remembered correctly from when they'd dated fifteen years before, it had a deck off the back that over-looked a large pond. "I heard about your father. I'd have been at the funeral, but I was on vacation when it happened. I didn't find out until I came home a week afterwards."

"He went fast and didn't suffer much. I didn't get to say good-bye..." Ian swallowed hard.

She fixed her gaze on the lower half of his face, the only part she could see. For a few seconds his lips, frowning, drew her total attention. Memories of that mouth kissing her flooded her mind, and her heart rate accelerated. "I'm sorry. He was a good man."

"The best."

"The last I heard you were working in Houston for the FBI. What made you come home now and run the ranch?" Now, when it was too late for them? Now, when her heart had finally scarred over where he'd broken it in two. And why did she care, anyway? It had been fifteen years.

"I promised my dad I wouldn't sell the ranch. It seemed appropriate I carry on for him."

"He had the best rodeo horses in this part of Texas, maybe in the whole state."

"Which may be a reason someone took Thunder. He's sired many champions."

Thunder, his stallion. That's why she was here at the Shamrock Ranch. She had to find out what she needed and leave. "When was the last time you saw him?"

"Last night about eleven."

"You were at the barn late?"

"No, looking out my office window. It gives me a good view of Thunder, the barn, and some of the fields where the mares are. There's a security light that shines on the barnyard and into the front of the paddock. He was at the fence."

"So he was taken between eleven and six. Did anything unusual happen in the middle of the night? Did you hear anything out of the ordinary?"

"Frisky barked"—he paused and tilted his head—"about two this morning. But Dad's dog does that most nights. I tune him out unless he persists. He didn't."

"Where's Frisky?"

Ian scowled. "At the vet's. Whoever took Thunder poisoned him. Doc Miller is keeping him overnight, but he should recover."

Sarah started for the gate into the paddock. "I'm going to take a look around."

"I already have. There are boot prints. There was only one set I couldn't rule out—size twelve or thirteen."

"One person? Are you sure?"

Finally Ian pushed his hat's brim up his forehead so she could clearly see his expression. "I might have left the FBI, but I've been a law enforcement officer at least two years longer than you. Also, I'm usually the only one who handles Thunder. It took me several months to come to a truce with the stallion."

"Temperamental?"

He nodded, removing his cowboy hat and raking his fingers through his thick brown hair. "Until he accepted me, my dad was the only one who dealt with him. That's why I'm surprised someone snuck into his pasture, grabbed him, and got away without Thunder making a lot of ruckus."

"If they poisoned Frisky, maybe they did something to Thunder to make him more docile."

"I suppose the person could have tranquilized him." Ian pointed to the boot prints near the railing by the gate. "As you can see, a truck pulling a trailer was backed up to this area."

"No ransom demand yet?"

"I wish. Then I would know Thunder might be returned. I haven't heard anything. If he isn't found, it will set the ranch back financially."

"Does anyone hold a grudge against you?" Besides me. But even she didn't, not really when she thought about why they'd parted years ago. She couldn't fulfill his dream of being in the FBI and making a difference, especially in keeping this country safe from terrorists. His best friend had died in a terrorist attack, an attack that haunted Ian. He was supposed to be at the courthouse in Dallas that day. But he'd been delayed.

After that, Ian was driven to stop terrorists from attacking innocent people. And in the process, he'd probably earned himself an enemy or two.

"I've put my fair share behind bars, but most of them are still in prison."

Sarah used her cell to snap some pictures of anything that might be evidence, but she had to agree with Ian. There wasn't much to go on. After she made a cast of the shoe print Ian had indicated didn't belong, her gaze connected with his. He had a way of looking at a person and making her feel possessed by him, as though he could read her mind.

She blinked and looked at his hat, his T-shirt, the ground, until she got her bearings back. Only then did she peer at his face again. "So no other horses or cattle are missing, just Thunder?"

One corner of his mouth hiked up. "That's what I said. If I remember anything else, I'll let you know."

"Please do. If it's the cattle-rustling group, stealing Thunder may mean they're branching out. He isn't an ordinary horse, but a prize stallion." She dug into the pocket of her tan pants and pulled out a business card, then wrote her cell number on the back of it. "It's easier to get a hold of me through my cell phone. I'm not in the office much. I have several counties to cover, so I'm on the road a lot. If they contact you about a ransom demand, please let me know. Do you have a photo of Thunder?"

"Come up to the house. I have one in my office. Thunder has a microchip injected in him to help identify him, so even if they change his outer appearance, we'll know when we've got him. But the scanner used to ID the horse has to be close to pick up the signal. No GPS tracking yet." Ian shut the gate and walked toward his house. "I've contacted the Equine Protection Registry, and he was put on their Hot List, which goes out to various agencies. The microchip can't be removed without surgery."

"Too bad about the GPS."

"Yeah, I know. One day that will be available, but that doesn't help me now. I had a tag with a GPS tracking system on Thunder, but I found it by the gate, smashed. If they try to take Thunder out of the country through legal channels, I might get him back. But I think he'll stay in the U.S. The rodeo circuit is strong, and a good horse is valuable."

"Some ranchers have microchips in their cattle. Our modern day branding. But there is a black market for cattle. A person can make good money with the price of beef so high." Sarah studied the tire tracks leading away from the gate. "How many people do you have working for you?"

"Two hands that have been with the ranch for years—Charlie and Tony. They aren't involved."

"Charlie was here when you and I…" For some reason the word dated wouldn't get past the lump lodged in her throat.

A few seconds passed before Ian said, "Yeah. Tony was hired five years ago. There were other cowhands, but they haven't been here since Dad cut back on the number of cattle last year." Ian opened the back door and waited for her to go inside first.

Stepping into the kitchen, she felt as if she'd stepped back in time. She and Ian would come in after riding and grab something cold to drink. Her gaze strayed to the same oak table in the alcove where she would sit with Ian right next to her and dream of the future. The memory sent her pulse rate up a notch.

Ian gestured toward the office down the hall, the same one his dad used for years. "Make yourself comfortable. I won't be long."

As she made her way toward the office, she could feel Ian's stare on her, but there was no way she would look back to see if she was correct. She hadn't been enough for him all those years ago. She'd been finishing her senior year in high school when he'd left the small junior college nearby. She'd been planning on going to school with him, but he'd been driven to seek his own path—without her.

Inside the office she strolled around, taking in what was new and what was old. A photo of him on his horse graced the wall behind the large desk. There was a time he'd thought that horse would be his partner on the rodeo circuit. That had been important to him once, but he'd discarded that dream, too. She paused at the window and glanced out, noting Thunder's paddock and the barn, just like he'd said.

Why had Ian come home now, after all this time? He promised his dad he would run the ranch, but the Ian she had known wouldn't have given up on his dreams for anyone. He sure hadn't given them up for her. Why did he leave the FBI for his father after his death? And why now?

11

DEADLY HOLIDAY

Book 3 in
Strong Women, Extraordinary Situations
by Margaret Daley

Tory Caldwell witnesses a hit-and-run, but when the dead victim disappears from the scene, police doubt a crime has been committed. Tory is threatened when she keeps insisting she saw a man killed and the only one who believes her is her neighbor, Jordan Steele. Together, can they solve the mystery of the disappearing body and stay alive?

DEADLY COUNTDOWN

Book 4 in
Strong Women, Extraordinary Situations
by Margaret Daley

Allie Martin, a widow, has a secret protector who manipulates her life without anyone knowing until...

When Remy Broussard, an injured police officer, returns to Port David, Louisiana to visit before his medical leave is over, he discovers his childhood friend, Allie Martin, is being stalked. As Remy protects Allie and tries to find her stalker, they realize their feelings go beyond friendship.

When the stalker is found, they begin to explore the deeper feelings they have for each other, only to have a more sinister threat come between them. Will Allie be able to save Remy before he dies at the hand of a maniac?

DEADLY NOEL

Book 5 in
Strong Women, Extraordinary Situations
by Margaret Daley

District attorney, Kira Davis, convicted the wrong man—Gabriel Michaels, a single dad with a young daughter. When new evidence was brought forth, his conviction was overturned, and Gabriel returned home to his ranch to put his life back together. Although Gabriel is free, the murderer of his wife is still out there and resumes killing women. In a desperate alliance, Kira and Gabriel join forces to find the true identity of the person terrorizing their town. Will they be able to forgive the past and find the killer before it's too late?

About the Author

Bestselling author, Margaret Daley, is multi-published with over 90 titles and 5 million books sold worldwide. She had written for Harlequin, Abingdon, Kensington, Dell, and Simon and Schuster. She has won multiple awards, including the prestigious Carol Award, Holt Medallion and Inspirational Readers' Choice Contest.

She has been married for over forty years and has one son and four granddaughters. When she isn't traveling, she's writing love stories, often with a suspense thread and corralling her three cats that think they rule her household.

To find out more about Margaret visit her website at *http://www.margaretdaley.com*.